GREAT EXPECTATIONS

THE GRAPHIC NOVEL
Charles Dickens

ORIGINAL TEXT VERSION

Script Adaptation: Jen Green
American English Adaptation: Joe Sutliff Sanders
Character Designs & Original Artwork: John Stokes
Coloring: Digikore Studios Ltd.
Color Finishing: Jason Cardy
Lettering: Jim Campbell
Design & Layout: Jo Wheeler & Jenny Placentino

Editor in Chief: Clive Bryant

Great Expectations: The Graphic Novel
Original Text Version

Charles Dickens

First US Edition

Published by: Classical Comics Ltd
Copyright ©2009 Classical Comics Ltd.

Acknowledgments: Every effort has been made to trace copyright holders of
material reproduced in this book. Any rights not acknowledged here will be
acknowledged in subsequent editions if notice is given to Classical Comics Ltd.

All enquiries should be addressed to:
Classical Comics Ltd.
PO Box 7280
Litchborough
Towcester
NN12 9AR
United Kingdom
Tel: +44 (0)845 812 3000

info@classicalcomics.com
www.classicalcomics.com

ISBN: 978-1-906332-59-4

Printed in the USA

This book is printed by CG Book Printers using environmentally safe inks, on environmentally
friendly paper which is FSC (Forest Stewardship Council) certified (SW-COC-003110). This material
can be disposed of by recycling, incineration for energy recovery, composting and biodegradation.

The rights of Jen Green, John Stokes, Digikore Studios Ltd., Jason Cardy, Jim Campbell
and Joe Sutliff Sanders to be identified as the artists of this work have been asserted in accordance
with the Copyright, Designs and Patents Act 1988 sections 77 and 78.

Contents

Dramatis Personæ

Young Pip
An orphan who lives with his sister and her husband

Adult Pip

Miss Havisham
An eccentric rich lady

Abel Magwitch
An escaped convict

Older Magwitch

Joe Gargery
Pip's brother-in-law

Mrs. Joe Gargery
Wife of Joe Gargery, and Pip's sister

Young Estella
Adopted daughter of Miss Havisham

Adult Estella

Young Biddy
Granddaughter to Mr. Wopsle's great-aunt

Adult Biddy

Herbert Pocket
Son of Miss Havisham's cousin

4

Mr. Matthew Pocket
*Herbert's father
and Miss Havisham's cousin*

Sarah Pocket
Miss Havisham's cousin

Clara Barley
Fiancée to Herbert Pocket

Bentley Drummle
Student, taught by Matthew Pocket

Startop
Student, taught by Matthew Pocket

Mr. Jaggers
A lawyer from London

John Wemmick
Clerk to Mr. Jaggers

Aged Parent
Wemmick's father

Molly
Jaggers's housekeeper

Dolge Orlick
Works for Joe Gargery

Compeyson
A criminal

Mr. Pumblechook
Joe Gargery's uncle

Prologue

The year is 1812.

In the southeast corner of England, about thirty miles from the City of London, lies an area of marshland that separates the estuaries of the River Thames and the River Medway.

It's a cold, damp, and misty area, home only to wildlife. There are a small number of villages nearby where a few countryside dwellings can be found, along with merchant traders, blacksmith's forges, and pubs. There's also an old church that marks the end of life — before the desolate rough lands reach out towards the sea.

Far out from the shore lie floating prisons — converted warships called "hulks" — that remove criminals from the overcrowded jails and keep them well away from society, while they await transportation to Australia and Tasmania. Murderers are hanged; but these ship-bound convicts are still considered dangerous enough to be banished from Britain for life.

This marshland is truly a bleak and barren place — the sort of place where someone could go unnoticed for a very long time; and where someone could stay hidden for as long as they wanted to hide...

Editor's Note:
The text that appears in this adaptation has been rigorously and diligently checked back to the original Dickens novel. Misspelled words (such as "pint" instead of "point", opposite) that were used to imply an accent in the speaker are reproduced in this adaptation, to remain true to the author's intentions.

MY FATHER'S FAMILY NAME BEING **PIRRIP**, AND MY CHRISTIAN NAME **PHILIP**, MY INFANT TONGUE COULD MAKE OF BOTH NAMES NOTHING LONGER OR MORE EXPLICIT THAN PIP. SO I CALLED MYSELF **PIP**.

I NEVER **SAW** MY FATHER OR MY MOTHER, AND NEVER SAW ANY **LIKENESS** OF **EITHER** OF THEM – OR MY FIVE LITTLE BROTHERS – FOR THEIR DAYS WERE **LONG** BEFORE THE DAYS OF PHOTOGRAPHS.

I FOUND OUT FOR CERTAIN THAT **THIS** BLEAK PLACE WAS THE CHURCHYARD; AND THAT PHILIP PIRRIP, LATE OF THIS PARISH, AND ALSO GEORGIANA, WIFE OF THE ABOVE, WERE **DEAD** AND **BURIED**.

AND THAT ALEXANDER, BARTHOLOMEW, ABRAHAM, TOBIAS AND ROGER, INFANT **CHILDREN** OF THE AFORESAID, WERE **ALSO** DEAD AND BURIED...

...AND THAT THE SMALL BUNDLE OF **SHIVERS** GROWING AFRAID OF IT ALL AND BEGINNING TO **CRY**, WAS PIP...

GASP!

HOLD YOUR NOISE!

KEEP **STILL**, YOU LITTLE **DEVIL**, OR I'LL CUT YOUR **THROAT**!

OH! **DON'T** CUT MY THROAT! **PRAY** DON'T DO IT, SIR!

TELL US YOUR **NAME**... QUICK!

PIP, SIR.

SHOW US WHERE YOU **LIVE**. PINT **OUT** THE PLACE!

AFTER AN HOUR OR SO OF TRAVELLING, WE CAME TO A ROUGH WOODEN HUT AND A LANDING-PLACE.

I WISH TO **SAY** SOMETHING RESPECTING THIS **ESCAPE.**

A MAN CAN'T **STARVE.** I **TOOK** SOME WITTLES, UP AT THE WILLAGE OVER YONDER – FROM THE **BLACKSMITH'S.**

MY WIFE SAW THEY WERE **MISSING.**

SO **YOU'RE** THE BLACKSMITH, ARE YOU? THEN I'M **SORRY** TO SAY, I'VE EAT YOUR **PIE.**

GOD KNOWS YOU'RE **WELCOME** TO IT – SO FAR AS IT WAS EVER MINE.

WE DON'T KNOW WHAT YOU HAVE **DONE,** BUT WE WOULDN'T HAVE YOU **STARVED** TO DEATH FOR IT, WOULD US, PIP?

VOLUME I
CHAPTER VI

BY THE LIGHT OF THE TORCHES, WE SAW THE **BLACK HULK** LYING OUT A LITTLE WAY FROM THE MUD OF THE SHORE, LIKE A WICKED NOAH'S ARK.

WE SAW HIM TAKEN UP THE SIDE AND DISAPPEAR. THEN THE ENDS OF THE TORCHES WERE FLUNG **HISSING** INTO THE WATER, AND WENT OUT, AS IF IT WERE **ALL OVER** WITH HIM.

I HAD BEEN EXONERATED, BUT IT DID NOT **IMPEL** ME TO FRANK DISCLOSURE FOR **FEAR** OF LOSING JOE'S **CONFIDENCE.**

MR. WOPSLE'S GREAT-AUNT KEPT AN EVENING SCHOOL IN THE VILLAGE. SHE WAS A **RIDICULOUS** OLD WOMAN, WHO USED TO GO TO SLEEP FROM SIX TO SEVEN EVERY EVENING, IN THE SOCIETY OF YOUTH WHO PAID TWO PENCE PER WEEK, FOR THE OPPORTUNITY OF SEEING HER DO IT.

MORE BY THE HELP OF BIDDY THAN MR. WOPSLE'S GREAT-AUNT, I STRUGGLED THROUGH THE ALPHABET. **BIDDY** WAS MR. WOPSLE'S GREAT-AUNT'S GRANDDAUGHTER. SHE WAS AN **ORPHAN** LIKE **MYSELF**; LIKE ME, TOO, SHE HAD BEEN BROUGHT UP BY HAND.

ONE NIGHT I WAS SITTING IN THE CHIMNEY CORNER WITH MY SLATE, EXPENDING **GREAT** EFFORTS ON THE PRODUCTION OF A LETTER TO JOE.

Mi deer Jo i ope
u r kr wite well
i ope i shal son b
habell 4 2 teedge
u jo an then we shofl
b so glodd an weni m
prengtd 2 u Jo
wot larx an
bleve me
inf xn
PiP

I SAY, PIP, OLD CHAP! WHY, HERE'S A J, AND A J-O, JOE. **ASTONISHING!** YOU **ARE** A **SCHOLAR**.

LIKE STEAM, JOE'S EDUCATION WAS YET IN ITS INFANCY. I OFFERED TO TEACH HIM MORE LETTERS.

NOW, WHEN YOU TAKE ME IN HAND IN MY LEARNING, PIP (AND I TELL YOU BEFOREHAND I AM **AWFUL** DULL), MRS. JOE MUSTN'T SEE TOO MUCH OF WHAT WE'RE **UP** TO.

SHE WOULD **NOT** BE OVER PARTIAL TO MY BEING A **SCHOLAR**, FOR FEAR AS I MIGHT **RISE**. LIKE A SORT OF **REBEL**, DON'T YOU SEE?

DON'T **DENY** THAT YOUR SISTER DROPS DOWN UPON US **HEAVY**. WHY DON'T I **RISE?** WELL, YOUR SISTER'S A MASTER-MIND. AND I **AIN'T** A MASTER-MIND.

LAST OF ALL, PIP, I WISH THERE **WARN'T** NO **TICKLER** FOR YOU, OLD CHAP; I WISH I COULD TAKE IT ALL ON MYSELF;

HOWEVER, HERE'S THE DUTCH CLOCK A WORKING HIMSELF UP TO STRIKE **EIGHT** OF 'EM, AND SHE'S NOT HOME YET.

VOLUME I
CHAPTER VIII

THE NEXT MORNING, MR. PUMBLECHOOK AND I BREAKFASTED AND AT TEN O'CLOCK WE STARTED FOR MISS HAVISHAM'S.

WITHIN A QUARTER OF AN HOUR WE CAME TO THE HOUSE. AFTER RINGING THE BELL, WE **WAITED** AT THE GATE.

THIS IS PIP.

THIS IS **PIP**, IS IT? COME **IN**, PIP.

DON'T **LOITER**, BOY.

ESTELLA WON THE GAME, AND I DEALT. I MISDEALT, AND SHE DENOUNCED ME FOR A STUPID, CLUMSY LABOURING-BOY.

YOU SAY **NOTHING** OF HER. SHE SAYS **MANY** HARD THINGS OF YOU.

WHAT DO YOU **THINK** OF HER? TELL ME IN MY EAR.

I think she is very *proud*... I think she is very *pretty*. And she is *very insulting*.

ANYTHING ELSE?

I think I should like to go *home*.

YOU SHALL GO **SOON**. PLAY THE GAME OUT.

I PLAYED THE GAME TO AN **END** WITH ESTELLA, AND SHE **BEGGARED** ME. SHE THREW THE CARDS DOWN ON THE TABLE AS IF SHE **DESPISED** THEM.

WHEN SHALL I HAVE YOU HERE AGAIN? LET ME THINK.

COME AGAIN AFTER **SIX DAYS**.

ESTELLA, TAKE HIM DOWN. LET HIM HAVE SOMETHING TO EAT, AND LET HIM LOOK ABOUT HIM WHILE HE EATS.

I FOLLOWED THE CANDLE DOWN, AS I HAD FOLLOWED THE CANDLE UP. AS ESTELLA OPENED THE SIDE ENTRANCE, THE RUSH OF THE DAYLIGHT QUITE **CONFOUNDED** ME.

YOU ARE TO WAIT HERE, YOU BOY.

SHE DISAPPEARED AND CLOSED THE DOOR. ALONE IN THE COURT-YARD, I LOOKED AT MY COARSE HANDS AND MY COMMON BOOTS. THEY HAD NEVER TROUBLED ME BEFORE, BUT THEY TROUBLED ME NOW; AS VULGAR APPENDAGES.

SHE CAME BACK, WITH SOME BREAD AND MEAT AND A LITTLE MUG OF BEER. SHE GAVE IT TO ME WITHOUT LOOKING AT ME, AS IF I WERE A DOG IN DISGRACE.

I WAS SO HUMILIATED AND HURT THAT I HAD TO HOLD BACK MY TEARS.

BUT WHEN SHE WAS **GONE**, I **HID** MY FACE AND **CRIED**.

I GOT RID OF MY **INJURED FEELINGS** FOR THE TIME, AND AFTER THE FOOD AND DRINK I WAS SOON IN SPIRITS TO LOOK ABOUT ME.

I ENTERED A GARDEN, OVERGROWN WITH TANGLED WEEDS, AND THERE FOUND AN OLD BREWERY; TO BE SURE, IT WAS A **DESERTED** PLACE.

BREWERY

AS I TURNED MY EYES TOWARDS A GREAT WOODEN BEAM, I SAW A FIGURE HANGING BY THE NECK.

AND THE FACE WAS **MISS HAVISHAM'S**.

WHEN I REACHED HOME, MR. PUMBLECHOOK WAS THERE. JOE WAS BUSY IN THE FORGE. MY SISTER WAS **VERY** CURIOUS TO KNOW ALL ABOUT MISS HAVISHAM'S, AND ASKED A NUMBER OF **QUESTIONS**. I FELT CONVINCED THAT IF I **DESCRIBED** MISS HAVISHAM'S AS MY EYES HAD SEEN IT, I SHOULD **NOT** BE UNDERSTOOD.

VOLUME I
CHAPTER IX

WELL, BOY, HOW DID YOU GET ON UP TOWN?

PRETTY WELL, SIR.

PRETTY WELL IS NO **ANSWER**. NOW, BOY! **WHAT** WAS MISS HAVISHAM A **DOING** OF, WHEN YOU WENT IN TODAY?

SHE WAS SITTING IN A BLACK VELVET COACH.

MISS ESTELLA – THAT'S HER **NIECE**, I THINK – HANDED HER IN **CAKE** AND **WINE** AT THE COACH-WINDOW, ON A **GOLD** PLATE. WE **ALL** HAD CAKE AND WINE ON GOLD PLATES. THERE WERE FOUR IMMENSE DOGS. AND THEY FOUGHT FOR VEAL-CUTLETS OUT OF A SILVER BASKET.

IN A BLACK VELVET COACH? CAN THIS BE **POSSIBLE**, UNCLE? WHAT CAN THE BOY MEAN?

MY OPINION, MUM, IS, IT'S A SEDAN-CHAIR. SHE'S **FLIGHTY**, YOU KNOW – QUITE FLIGHTY ENOUGH TO PASS HER DAYS IN A SEDAN-CHAIR.

WHEN JOE CAME IN FROM HIS WORK, MY SISTER RELATED MY PRETENDED EXPERIENCES. NOW, WHEN I SAW JOE OPEN HIS EYES IN HELPLESS AMAZEMENT, I WAS OVERTAKEN BY **PENITENCE**.

MRS. JOE AND MR. PUMBLECHOOK SAT DEBATING WHAT RESULTS WOULD COME FROM MISS HAVISHAM'S **FAVOUR**. THEY HAD NO DOUBT THAT MISS HAVISHAM WOULD "**DO SOMETHING**" FOR ME.

AFTER MR. PUMBLECHOOK HAD DRIVEN OFF, I STOLE INTO THE FORGE TO JOE.

JOE, I SHOULD LIKE TO **TELL** YOU SOMETHING. YOU REMEMBER ALL THAT ABOUT MISS HAVISHAM'S?

IT'S A TERRIBLE THING, BUT IT AIN'T **TRUE**. IT'S **LIES**, JOE.

NOT **ALL** OF IT? PIP, OLD CHAP!

I SAY! THAT'S **AWFUL**! WHAT **POSSESSED** YOU?

THEN I TOLD JOE THAT I FELT VERY **MISERABLE**, AND HOW I WISHED I WAS NOT **COMMON**, AND THE LIES HAD COME OF IT SOMEHOW.

LIES IS **LIES**. HOWSEVER THEY COME, THEY DIDN'T OUGHT TO COME. AND AS TO BEING COMMON, I DON'T MAKE IT OUT. YOU ARE ONCOMMON IN SOME THINGS. YOU'RE ONCOMMON **SMALL**. LIKEWISE YOU'RE A ONCOMMON **SCHOLAR**.

NO, I AM IGNORANT AND **BACKWARD**, JOE.

WELL, PIP, BE IT SO OR BE IT SON'T, YOU MUST BE A COMMON SCHOLAR **AFORE** YOU CAN BE A ONCOMMON ONE! THE KING **CAN'T** WRITE HIS ACTS OF PARLIAMENT, WITHOUT HAVING BEGUN, WHEN HE WAS A PRINCE, WITH THE **ALPHABET**.

THERE WAS SOME **HOPE** IN THIS PIECE OF WISDOM.

THE IDEA OCCURRED TO ME THAT THE **BEST** STEP I COULD TAKE TOWARDS MAKING MYSELF UNCOMMON WAS TO GET OUT OF BIDDY **EVERYTHING** SHE KNEW. I MENTIONED TO HER THAT I HAD A PARTICULAR **REASON** FOR WISHING TO **GET ON** IN LIFE.

VOLUME I
CHAPTER X

I TOLD BIDDY THAT I SHOULD FEEL VERY MUCH OBLIGED TO HER IF SHE WOULD IMPART **ALL** HER LEARNING TO ME. BIDDY, WHO WAS THE MOST **OBLIGING** OF GIRLS, IMMEDIATELY SAID SHE **WOULD**, AND INDEED BEGAN TO CARRY OUT HER PROMISE WITHIN FIVE MINUTES.

THERE WAS A PUBLIC-HOUSE IN THE VILLAGE, AND JOE LIKED SOMETIMES TO SMOKE HIS PIPE THERE. I HAD RECEIVED **STRICT** ORDERS FROM MY SISTER TO CALL FOR HIM AT THE THREE JOLLY BARGEMEN ON MY WAY FROM SCHOOL, AND BRING HIM **HOME**.

I FOUND HIM IN THE COMMON ROOM, SMOKING HIS PIPE WITH MR. WOPSLE AND A **STRANGER**.

THE MOMENT JOE GREETED ME, THE STRANGER TURNED HIS HEAD AND **LOOKED** AT ME. HE WAS A SECRET-LOOKING MAN WHOM I HAD NEVER SEEN BEFORE. HE LOOKED HARD AT ME, NODDED, AND MADE ROOM ON THE SETTLE BESIDE HIM.

I WAS USED TO SIT BESIDE JOE, SO I FELL INTO THE SPACE BESIDE HIM. THE STRANGE MAN, AFTER GLANCING AT JOE, AND SEEING THAT HIS ATTENTION WAS ENGAGED, NODDED TO ME AGAIN, AND THEN RUBBED HIS **LEG** IN A VERY **ODD** WAY.

YOU WAS SAYING THAT YOU WAS A **BLACKSMITH?** WHAT'LL YOU DRINK, MR.-- GARGERY, IS IT?

AT MY EXPENSE?

I WOULDN'T WISH TO BE STIFF COMPANY! **RUM!**

THREE **RUMS!** GLASSES ROUND!

I AM NOT ACQUAINTED WITH THIS COUNTRY, GENTLEMEN, BUT IT SEEMS A **SOLITARY** COUNTRY TOWARDS THE RIVER.

MOST MARSHES **IS** SOLITARY. NONE BUT A RUNAWAY **CONVICT** NOW AND THEN, AND WE DON'T FIND THEM, **EASY**, EH, MR. WOPSLE?

SEEMS YOU HAVE BEEN **OUT** AFTER SUCH?

ONCE.

THE STRANGER LOOKED AT ME **AGAIN** -- STILL COCKING HIS EYE, AS IF HE WERE TAKING AIM AT ME WITH HIS INVISIBLE **GUN**.

HE'S A **LIKELY** YOUNG PARCEL OF BONES THAT. WHAT IS IT YOU CALL HIM?

PIP.

VOLUME I
CHAPTER XI

AT THE APPOINTED TIME I RETURNED TO MISS HAVISHAM'S. MY RING AT THE GATE BROUGHT ESTELLA, WHO LED ME TO QUITE **ANOTHER** PART OF THE HOUSE.

YOU ARE TO COME THIS WAY TODAY.

SHE LED ME ALONG DARK PASSAGES, AND OUT ACROSS A SMALL PAVED COURT-YARD, TO A DETACHED DWELLING-HOUSE. WE ENTERED A **GLOOMY** ROOM. THERE WAS SOME COMPANY IN THE ROOM, THREE LADIES AND A GENTLEMAN.

MY COMING **STOPPED** THE CONVERSATION, AND THE OTHER OCCUPANTS **LOOKED** AT ME.

YOU ARE TO GO AND STAND THERE, BOY, TILL YOU ARE **WANTED**.

THE THREE LADIES AND GENTLEMAN ALL HAD A **LISTLESS** AND **DREARY** AIR OF WAITING SOMEBODY'S **PLEASURE**.

POOR **DEAR** SOUL! MATTHEW IS NOBODY'S ENEMY BUT HIS **OWN**!

WE ARE TO LOVE OUR NEIGHBOUR.

POOR SOUL! HE IS SO VERY **STRANGE**!

DING A LING

NOW, BOY!

AS WE WERE GOING WITH OUR CANDLE ALONG THE DARK PASSAGE, ESTELLA **STOPPED** ALL OF A SUDDEN, AND FACED ME.

AM I **PRETTY**?

YES, I THINK YOU ARE **VERY** PRETTY.

AM I **INSULTING**?

NOT SO MUCH AS YOU WERE **LAST** TIME.

29

smack!

NOW, YOU LITTLE COARSE **MONSTER**, WHAT DO YOU THINK OF ME **NOW?**

I **SHALL** NOT TELL YOU.

WHICH WAS A FALSE DECLARATION AS **EVER** WAS MADE, FOR I WAS INWARDLY CRYING FOR HER THEN.

WHY DON'T YOU **CRY** AGAIN YOU LITTLE WRETCH?

BECAUSE I'LL **NEVER** CRY FOR YOU **AGAIN**.

AS WE WERE MAKING OUR WAY **UP** STAIRS, WE MET A GENTLEMAN GROPING HIS WAY **DOWN**.

WHOM HAVE WE HERE? BOY OF THE NEIGHBOURHOOD, HEY? HOW DO **YOU** COME **HERE?**

MISS HAVISHAM SENT FOR ME, SIR.

WELL! BEHAVE YOURSELF. I HAVE A PRETTY LARGE EXPERIENCE OF BOYS, AND YOU'RE A **BAD** SET OF FELLOWS. MIND YOU BEHAVE YOURSELF!

WITH THOSE WORDS, HE RELEASED ME. I WAS **GLAD**, FOR HIS HAND SMELT OF SCENTED SOAP. HE WENT HIS WAY DOWN STAIRS.

WE WERE SOON IN MISS HAVISHAM'S ROOM. ESTELLA LEFT ME STANDING NEAR THE DOOR.

ARE YOU READY TO **PLAY?**

I DON'T THINK I **AM**, MA'AM.

THEN ARE YOU WILLING TO **WORK?**

I AM QUITE WILLING.

THEN GO INTO THAT OPPOSITE ROOM, AND **WAIT** THERE TILL I COME.

30

I CROSSED THE LANDING, AND ENTERED THE DARK ROOM SHE INDICATED. IT WAS SPACIOUS, BUT EVERY DISCERNIBLE THING IN IT WAS COVERED WITH *DUST* AND *MOULD*, AND DROPPING TO PIECES.

THE MOST PROMINENT OBJECT WAS A LONG TABLE WITH A TABLECLOTH SPREAD ON IT, AS IF A FEAST HAD BEEN IN PREPARATION WHEN THE HOUSE AND THE CLOCKS ALL *STOPPED* TOGETHER.

A CENTRE-PIECE OF SOME KIND IN THE MIDDLE OF THE CLOTH WAS HEAVILY OVERHUNG WITH COBWEBS.

AS I LOOKED, I SAW SPECKLE-LEGGED SPIDERS WITH BLOTCHY BODIES RUNNING HOME TO IT, AND RUNNING OUT FROM IT.

THIS IS MY BIRTHDAY, PIP.

I DON'T SUFFER THOSE WHO WERE HERE JUST NOW TO **SPEAK** OF IT. ON THIS DAY OF THE YEAR, LONG BEFORE YOU WERE BORN, THIS HEAP OF DECAY WAS BROUGHT HERE.

IT AND I HAVE WORN AWAY **TOGETHER**. THE MICE HAVE GNAWED AT IT, AND SHARPER TEETH THAN TEETH OF **MICE** HAVE GNAWED AT **ME**.

SHE STOOD LOOKING AT THE TABLE, AND I REMAINED QUIET.

AT LENGTH, ESTELLA RETURNED, AND A DAY WAS APPOINTED FOR MY RETURN. THEN I WAS TAKEN DOWN INTO THE YARD TO BE **FED** IN THE FORMER DOG-LIKE MANNER.

THERE, TOO, I WAS AGAIN LEFT TO WANDER ABOUT AS I LIKED.

AFTER A STROLL AROUND THE GARDEN, WHICH WAS QUITE A **WILDERNESS**, I FOUND MYSELF BACK BY THE DISMAL HOUSE IN WHICH I HAD WAITED EARLIER. BELIEVING THAT THE HOUSE WAS NOW EMPTY, I LOOKED IN AT A WINDOW...

...AND SAW A PALE YOUNG GENTLEMAN, WHO QUICKLY **DISAPPEARED**...

...AND **REAPPEARED** BESIDE ME. HE HAD BEEN AT HIS BOOKS WHEN HE FOUND ME **STARING** AT HIM.

HALLOA, YOUNG FELLOW! WHO LET **YOU** IN AND GAVE YOU **LEAVE** TO **PROWL** ABOUT?

MISS ESTELLA.

COME AND FIGHT!

WHAT COULD I DO BUT **FOLLOW** HIM? HIS MANNER WAS SO **FINAL**, AND I WAS SO **ASTONISHED**, THAT I FOLLOWED WHERE HE LED.

AARRGH!

33

THE MORE I THOUGHT OF THE FIGHT, THE MORE CERTAIN IT APPEARED THAT **SOMETHING** WOULD BE DONE TO ME.

FOR SOME DAYS, I EVEN KEPT CLOSE AT HOME, AND LOOKED OUT AT THE KITCHEN DOOR WITH THE GREATEST **CAUTION** AND TREPIDATION BEFORE GOING ON AN ERRAND, LEST THE OFFICERS OF THE **COUNTY JAIL** SHOULD **POUNCE** UPON ME.

WHEN THE DAY CAME ROUND FOR MY **RETURN** TO THE SCENE OF THE DEED OF VIOLENCE, MY **TERRORS** REACHED THEIR **HEIGHT**.

HOWEVER, GO TO MISS HAVISHAM'S I **MUST**, AND GO I **DID**.

AND **BEHOLD!** NOTHING CAME OF THE LATE STRUGGLE. IT WAS NOT ALLUDED TO IN ANY WAY, AND NO PALE YOUNG GENTLEMAN WAS TO BE DISCOVERED ON THE PREMISES.

I ENTERED, THAT SAME DAY, ON A REGULAR OCCUPATION OF PUSHING MISS HAVISHAM ROUND HER OWN ROOM, AND ACROSS THE LANDING, AND ROUND THE OTHER ROOM.

OVER AND OVER AND OVER AGAIN, WE WOULD MAKE THESE JOURNEYS, AND SOMETIMES THEY WOULD LAST AS LONG AS THREE HOURS AT A STRETCH.

Does she grow **prettier** and **prettier** Pip?

Yes.

I SHOULD RETURN EVERY ALTERNATE DAY AT NOON FOR THESE PURPOSES, OVER A PERIOD OF AT LEAST **EIGHT** OR **TEN** MONTHS.

ESTELLA WAS ALWAYS ABOUT, BUT NEVER TOLD ME I MIGHT KISS HER AGAIN. SOMETIMES SHE WOULD COLDLY **TOLERATE** ME. SOMETIMES SHE WOULD **CONDESCEND** TO ME.

SOMETIMES SHE WOULD BE QUITE **FAMILIAR** WITH ME. SOMETIMES SHE WOULD TELL ME **ENERGETICALLY** THAT SHE **HATED** ME.

Break their **hearts** my pride and hope, break their hearts and have **no mercy!**

ON THE NEXT DAY BUT ONE, JOE ARRAYED HIMSELF IN HIS SUNDAY CLOTHES TO ACCOMPANY ME TO MISS HAVISHAM'S. THE FORGE WAS SHUT UP FOR THE DAY.

MY SISTER DECLARED HER INTENTION OF GOING TO TOWN WITH US, AND BEING LEFT AT UNCLE PUMBLECHOOK'S.

HOUT

AT MISS HAVISHAM'S HOUSE, *ESTELLA* OPENED THE GATE AS USUAL. SHE TOOK *NO NOTICE* OF *EITHER* OF US, BUT LED US THE WAY THAT I KNEW SO WELL.

YOU ARE *BOTH* TO GO IN.

THROUGHOUT THE INTERVIEW, JOE *PERSISTED* IN ADDRESSING *ME* INSTEAD OF MISS HAVISHAM...

YOU HAVE *REARED* THE BOY, WITH THE INTENTION OF TAKING HIM FOR YOUR *APPRENTICE;* IS THAT SO, MR. GARGERY?

AS YOU AND ME WERE EVER *FRIENDS,* IF YOU HAD EVER MADE *OBJECTIONS* TO THE BUSINESS, THEY WOULD HAVE BEEN *ATTENDED* TO.

HAVE YOU BROUGHT HIS INDENTURES *WITH* YOU?

WELL, *PIP,* YOU YOURSELF SEE ME PUT 'EM IN MY 'AT.

YOU EXPECTED NO *PREMIUM* WITH THE BOY?

PIP, WHICH I MEANTERSAY, YOU KNOW THE ANSWER TO BE FULL WELL NO, PIP.

PIP HAS EARNED A PREMIUM *HERE;* AND HERE IT IS. THERE ARE FIVE-AND-TWENTY GUINEAS IN THIS BAG. GIVE IT TO YOUR *MASTER,* PIP.

THIS IS WERY *LIBERAL* ON YOUR PART, PIP --

-- AND IT IS AS SUCH RECEIVED AND GRATEFUL WELCOME, THOUGH NEVER LOOKED FOR. AND NOW, OLD CHAP, MAY YOU AND ME DO OUR *DUTY;* BOTH ON US, BY ONE AND ANOTHER!

GOODBYE, PIP! LET THEM OUT, ESTELLA.

AM I TO COME *AGAIN,* MISS HAVISHAM?

NO. *GARGERY* IS YOUR *MASTER* NOW.

37

WELL? AND WHAT'S **HAPPENED** TO YOU?

MISS HAVISHAM MADE IT **WERY** PARTICK'LER THAT WE SHOULD GIVE HER **COMPLIMENTS** TO MRS. J. GARGERY--

MUCH GOOD **THEY'LL** DO ME! AND WHAT DID SHE **GIVE** YOUNG RANTIPOLE HERE?

SHE GIV' HIM **NOTHING.**

WHAT SHE GIV', SHE GIV' INTO THE HANDS OF HIS SISTER MRS. J. GARGERY - IT'S **FIVE-AND-TWENTY POUND!**

NOW YOU SEE, JOSEPH AND WIFE, I AM ONE OF THEM THAT **ALWAYS** GO RIGHT THROUGH WITH WHAT THEY'VE BEGUN. THIS BOY MUST BE **BOUND,** OUT OF HAND. THAT'S **MY WAY.**

THE JUSTICES WERE SITTING IN THE TOWN HALL NEAR AT HAND, AND WE AT ONCE WENT OVER TO HAVE ME **BOUND APPRENTICE** TO JOE IN THE MAGISTERIAL PRESENCE.

What's **he** done?

He's a **young** 'un, too, but looks **bad** don't he?

TOWN HALL

MY SISTER BECAME SO EXCITED, THAT NOTHING WOULD SERVE HER BUT WE MUST HAVE A **DINNER** AT THE BLUE BOAR; A MOST **MELANCHOLY** DAY I PASSED.

THE SWINDLING PUMBLECHOOK TOOK THE **TOP** OF THE TABLE AND, WHEN HE ADDRESSED THEM ON THE SUBJECT OF MY BEING **BOUND,** HE PLACED ME ON A CHAIR BESIDE HIM.

THEY WOULDN'T LET ME GO TO **SLEEP.** WHENEVER THEY SAW ME DROPPING OFF, THEY WOKE ME UP AND TOLD ME TO **ENJOY** MYSELF.

WHEN I **FINALLY** GOT INTO MY LITTLE BEDROOM I WAS TRULY **WRETCHED,** AND HAD A STRONG CONVICTION THAT I SHOULD **NEVER** LIKE JOE'S TRADE.

I HAD LIKED IT **ONCE,** BUT ONCE WAS NOT **NOW.**

IT IS A MOST **MISERABLE** THING TO FEEL **ASHAMED** OF HOME. I CAN TESTIFY. HOME HAD NEVER BEEN A VERY **PLEASANT** PLACE TO ME, BECAUSE OF MY SISTER'S **TEMPER**. BUT JOE HAD **SANCTIFIED** IT, AND I HAD **BELIEVED** IN IT.

VOLUME I
CHAPTER XIV

WITHIN A SINGLE YEAR ALL THIS WAS **CHANGED**. NOW IT WAS ALL **COARSE** AND **COMMON**.

I USED TO STAND ABOUT THE CHURCHYARD ON SUNDAY EVENINGS, COMPARING MY **OWN** PERSPECTIVE WITH THE FLAT, LOW MARSH VIEW. **WHAT** I WANTED, WHO CAN **SAY**?

WHAT I **DREADED** WAS, THAT IN SOME UNLUCKY HOUR I, BEING AT MY **GRIMIEST** AND **COMMONEST**, SHOULD LOOK UP AND SEE **ESTELLA** LOOKING IN AT THE FORGE. SHE WOULD FIND ME WITH A BLACK **FACE** AND **HANDS**, AND WOULD **DESPISE** ME.

VOLUME I
CHAPTER XV

AS I WAS GETTING TOO BIG FOR MR. WOPSLE'S GREAT-AUNT'S ROOM, MY EDUCATION UNDER THAT FEMALE **TERMINATED**.

NOT, HOWEVER, UNTIL BIDDY HAD IMPARTED TO ME EVERYTHING SHE **KNEW**. WHATEVER I ACQUIRED BY WAY OF EDUCATION FROM BIDDY, I TRIED TO IMPART TO **JOE**.

THIS STATEMENT SOUNDS WELL, BUT I DID IT TO MAKE JOE LESS IGNORANT AND COMMON, THAT HE MIGHT BE **WORTHIER** OF MY SOCIETY AND LESS OPEN TO ESTELLA'S **REPROACH**.

JOE, DON'T YOU THINK I **OUGHT** TO MAKE MISS HAVISHAM A **VISIT**?

WELL, PIP, WHAT **FOR**?

HERE AM I, GETTING ON IN THE FIRST YEAR OF MY TIME, AND I HAVE NEVER **THANKED** MISS HAVISHAM, OR SHOWN THAT I **REMEMBER** HER.

AS WE ARE RATHER SLACK JUST NOW, IF YOU WOULD GIVE ME A HALF-HOLIDAY TO-MORROW, I THINK I WOULD **GO** UP-TOWN AND MAKE A CALL ON MISS **EST**... HAVISHAM.

WHICH HER NAME **AIN'T ESTAVISHAM**, PIP, UNLESS SHE HAVE BEEN RECHRIS'ENED.

I **KNOW**, JOE, IT WAS A **SLIP** OF MINE. WHAT DO YOU THINK OF IT, JOE?

JOE THOUGHT **WELL** ENOUGH OF IT. BUT, HE WAS PARTICULAR IN STIPULATING THAT IF I WERE **NOT** RECEIVED WITH **CORDIALITY**, THIS TRIP SHOULD HAVE **NO SUCCESSOR**. BY THESE CONDITIONS I PROMISED TO **ABIDE**.

JOE KEPT A JOURNEYMAN AT WEEKLY WAGES WHOSE NAME WAS **DOLGE ORLICK**. HE WAS A FELLOW OF **OBSTINATE** DISPOSITION, AND ALWAYS SLOUCHING. THIS MOROSE JOURNEYMAN HAD NO LIKING FOR ME. WHEN I BECAME JOE'S 'PRENTICE, ORLICK WAS PERHAPS **CONFIRMED** IN THE SUSPICION THAT I SHOULD **DISPLACE** HIM.

NOW MASTER, SURE YOU'RE NOT A-GOING TO FAVOUR ONLY **ONE** OF US. IF YOUNG PIP HAS A HALF-HOLIDAY, DO AS MUCH FOR OLD **ORLICK**.

WHY, WHAT'LL **YOU** DO WITH A HALF-HOLIDAY, IF YOU GET IT?

WHAT'LL I DO WITH IT! I'LL DO AS **MUCH** WITH IT AS **HIM**.

IF YOUNG PIP'S A GOING UP-TOWN, OLD ORLICK, HE'S A GOING UP-TOWN. NOW, MASTER! NO FAVOURING IN THIS SHOP. BE A **MAN**!

THEN, AS IN **GENERAL** YOU STICK TO YOUR **WORK** AS WELL AS **MOST** MEN, LET IT BE A HALF-HOLIDAY FOR **ALL**.

YOU **FOOL**! GIVING **HOLIDAYS** TO GREAT IDLE **HULKERS** LIKE THAT!

YOU ARE A **RICH** MAN, UPON MY LIFE, TO WASTE WAGES IN THAT WAY! I WISH **I** WAS HIS **MASTER**!

YOU'D BE **EVERYBODY'S** MASTER, IF YOU DURST.

LET HER ALONE.

I'D BE A **MATCH** FOR ALL **NOODLES** AND ALL **ROGUES**!

AND I **COULDN'T** BE A MATCH FOR **ROGUES**, WITHOUT BEING A MATCH FOR **YOU**, WHO ARE THE **WORST** ROGUE BETWEEN **THIS** AND **FRANCE**!

YOU'RE A **FOUL SHREW**, MOTHER GARGERY.

IF THAT MAKES A **JUDGE** OF **ROGUES**, YOU OUGHT TO BE A **GOOD'UN**.

40

THWAAKK!

JOE PICKED UP MY SISTER WHO HAD DROPPED **INSENSIBLE** TO THE FLOOR. SHE WAS CARRIED INTO THE HOUSE TO **REVIVE**.
I WENT UP-STAIRS TO DRESS MYSELF.

WHEN I CAME DOWN AGAIN, I FOUND JOE AND ORLICK SWEEPING UP, WITHOUT **ANY TRACES** OF DISCOMPOSURE.

WITH WHAT **ABSURD** EMOTIONS I FOUND MYSELF AGAIN GOING TO MISS HAVISHAM'S, MATTERS **LITTLE**.

MISS SARAH POCKET LET ME IN, AND BROUGHT THE MESSAGE THAT I WAS TO "COME UP". EVERYTHING WAS **UNCHANGED**, AND MISS HAVISHAM WAS **ALONE**. THERE WAS NO **ESTELLA**.

YOU ARE LOOKING ROUND FOR **ESTELLA?**

I H-H-HOPE THAT SHE IS W-W-WELL.

ABROAD, EDUCATING FOR A **LADY**. **FAR** OUT OF REACH. DO YOU FEEL THAT YOU HAVE **LOST** HER? Heh-heh-heh...

I WAS AT A **LOSS** WHAT TO SAY. SHE SPARED ME THE TROUBLE OF CONSIDERING, BY **DISMISSING** ME.

WHEN THE GATE WAS CLOSED ON ME, I FELT MORE THAN EVER **DISSATISFIED** WITH MY **HOME** AND WITH MY **TRADE** AND WITH **EVERYTHING**.

41

I WAS LOITERING ALONG THE HIGH STREET WHEN I MET WITH MR. WOPSLE, WHO *INSISTED* ON MY ACCOMPANYING HIM TO SEE UNCLE PUMBLECHOOK. IT WAS A *VERY* DARK NIGHT BY THE TIME WE SET OUT ON THE WALK HOME.

HALLOA! ORLICK, THERE?

AH! I WAS STANDING BY, A MINUTE, ON THE *CHANCE* OF COMPANY.

THE *GUNS* IS GOING AGAIN. THERE'S SOME *JAIL-BIRDS* FLOWN FROM THE *HULKS.*

WE CAME TO THE VILLAGE BY WAY OF THE JOLLY BARGEMEN, WHICH WE WERE SURPRISED TO FIND IN A STATE OF *COMMOTION.* MR. WOPSLE DROPPED IN TO ASK WHAT WAS THE MATTER BUT CAME RUNNING OUT IN A GREAT *HURRY.*

THERE'S SOMETHING *WRONG* UP AT YOUR PLACE, PIP!

THE HOUSE SEEMS TO HAVE BEEN *VIOLENTLY* ENTERED WHEN JOE WAS OUT.

SOMEBODY HAS BEEN *ATTACKED* AND *HURT.*

RUN ALL!

OUR KITCHEN WAS FULL OF PEOPLE, AND THERE WAS A *SURGEON.*

MY SISTER WAS LYING WITHOUT SENSE OR MOVEMENT ON THE BARE BOARDS WHERE SHE HAD BEEN KNOCKED DOWN BY A *TREMENDOUS* BLOW ON THE BACK OF THE *HEAD,* DEALT BY SOME *UNKNOWN* HAND.

ON THE GROUND BESIDE HER WAS A *LEG-IRON* WHICH HAD BEEN FILED ASUNDER SOME TIME AGO.

I BELIEVED IT TO BE MY **CONVICT'S** IRON – BUT I BELIEVED NOT **HE**, BUT ONE OF TWO **OTHER** PERSONS TO HAVE TURNED IT TO THIS CRUEL ACCOUNT. EITHER **ORLICK**, OR THE **STRANGE MAN** WITH THE FILE.

THE CONSTABLES AND BOW STREET MEN FROM LONDON WERE ABOUT THE HOUSE FOR A WEEK OR TWO. THEY STOOD ABOUT THE DOOR OF THE JOLLY BARGEMEN WITH KNOWING LOOKS.

THEY HAD A MYSTERIOUS MANNER OF TAKING THEIR DRINK, THAT WAS ALMOST AS GOOD AS TAKING THE CULPRIT. BUT NOT QUITE, FOR THEY NEVER DID IT.

LONG AFTER THESE POWERS HAD **DISPERSED**, MY SISTER LAY ILL IN BED. HER **SIGHT** WAS DISTURBED, HER **HEARING** IMPAIRED, HER **MEMORY** ALSO; AND HER SPEECH WAS **UNINTELLIGIBLE**.

WHEN AT LAST SHE COULD BE HELPED DOWN STAIRS, IT WAS NECESSARY TO KEEP MY SLATE BY HER, THAT SHE MIGHT INDICATE IN **WRITING** WHAT SHE COULD NOT IN **SPEECH**.

HOWEVER, HER **TEMPER** WAS GREATLY **IMPROVED**, AND SHE WAS **PATIENT**.

WE WERE AT A LOSS TO FIND A SUITABLE ATTENDANT FOR HER, UNTIL MR. WOPSLE'S GREAT-AUNT DIED, AND **BIDDY** BECAME A PART OF OUR **HOUSEHOLD**.

SHE QUICKLY BECAME A **BLESSING** TO US, AND ABOVE ALL, TO JOE, WHO WAS SADLY CUT UP.

VOLUME I
CHAPTER XVIII

IT WAS IN THE FOURTH YEAR OF MY APPRENTICESHIP TO JOE, AND A SATURDAY NIGHT. THERE WAS A GROUP OF US ASSEMBLED ROUND THE FIRE AT THE JOLLY BARGEMEN, ATTENTIVE TO MR. WOPSLE AS HE READ THE NEWSPAPER ALOUD.

I BECAME AWARE OF A STRANGE GENTLEMAN LEANING OVER THE BACK OF THE SETTLE OPPOSITE, LOOKING ON WITH AN EXPRESSION OF **CONTEMPT**.

THE STRANGE GENTLEMAN WENT AND STOOD BY THE FIRE. HE DID NOT RECOGNISE **ME**, BUT I RECOGNISED **HIM** AS THE GENTLEMAN I HAD MET ON THE STAIRS, ON MY SECOND VISIT TO MISS HAVISHAM.

FROM INFORMATION I HAVE RECEIVED, I HAVE REASON TO BELIEVE THERE IS A **BLACKSMITH** AMONG YOU, BY NAME JOSEPH – OR JOE – GARGERY. WHICH IS THE MAN?

HERE IS THE MAN.

YOU HAVE AN APPRENTICE, COMMONLY KNOWN AS **PIP**? IS HE **HERE**?

I AM HERE!

I WISH TO HAVE A **PRIVATE** CONFERENCE WITH YOU TWO. IT WILL TAKE A LITTLE TIME. PERHAPS WE HAD BETTER GO TO YOUR PLACE OF **RESIDENCE**.

AMIDST A **WONDERING SILENCE**, WE WALKED OUT OF THE JOLLY BARGEMEN, AND IN A **WONDERING SILENCE** WALKED **HOME**.

NOW, MR. PIP. YOU ARE TO UNDERSTAND, FIRST, THAT IT IS THE REQUEST OF THE PERSON FROM WHOM I TAKE MY INSTRUCTIONS THAT YOU **ALWAYS** BEAR THE NAME OF **PIP.**

YOU HAVE NO **OBJECTION** TO YOUR GREAT EXPECTATIONS BEING ENCUMBERED WITH THAT **EASY** CONDITION?

N...N...N...NO.

I SHOULD THINK **NOT!**

MY HEART WAS BEATING SO **FAST** THAT I COULD SCARCELY STAMMER.

YOU ARE TO UNDERSTAND, SECONDLY, THAT THE **NAME** OF THE PERSON WHO IS YOUR LIBERAL BENEFACTOR REMAINS A PROFOUND **SECRET,** UNTIL THE PERSON **CHOOSES** TO **REVEAL** IT AT FIRST HAND.

WHEN THAT INTENTION MAY BE CARRIED OUT, I CANNOT SAY; IT MAY BE **YEARS** HENCE.

NOW, YOU ARE MOST POSITIVELY **PROHIBITED** FROM MAKING **ANY** INQUIRY ON THIS HEAD, OR ANY ALLUSION OR REFERENCE, IN THE COMMUNICATIONS YOU MAY HAVE WITH ME.

IF YOU HAVE A **SUSPICION,** KEEP IT IN YOUR OWN BREAST. AGAIN, NOT A VERY **DIFFICULT** CONDITION, MR. PIP, BUT IF YOU HAVE ANY OBJECTION TO IT, **THIS** IS THE TIME TO SPEAK OUT.

N...N...N...NO.

WE COME NEXT, TO THE **DETAILS** OF ARRANGEMENT. YOU ARE NOT ENDOWED WITH EXPECTATIONS **ONLY.** THERE IS ALREADY LODGED IN MY HANDS A SUM OF **MONEY** AMPLY SUFFICIENT FOR YOUR SUITABLE EDUCATION AND MAINTENANCE.

YOU WILL PLEASE CONSIDER ME YOUR **GUARDIAN.** IT IS CONSIDERED THAT YOU MUST BE BETTER **EDUCATED,** IN ACCORDANCE WITH YOUR ALTERED POSITION.

I HAVE **ALWAYS** LONGED FOR IT.

NOW, THERE IS A CERTAIN TUTOR, OF WHOM I HAVE SOME KNOWLEDGE, WHO I THINK MIGHT SUIT THE **PURPOSE.**

I DON'T **RECOMMEND** HIM, OBSERVE; BECAUSE I NEVER RECOMMEND ANYBODY. THE GENTLEMAN I SPEAK OF IS ONE **MR. MATTHEW POCKET.**

AH!

I **CAUGHT** AT THE NAME DIRECTLY. MISS HAVISHAM'S **RELATION.** THE MATTHEW WHOM MRS. CAMILLA HAD SPOKEN OF, WHOSE PLACE WAS TO BE AT MISS HAVISHAM'S **HEAD,** WHEN SHE LAY DEAD.

YOU HAD BETTER TRY HIM IN HIS OWN HOUSE. YOU CAN SEE HIS SON FIRST, WHO IS IN **LONDON.**

WHEN WILL YOU COME TO LONDON?

I SUPPOSE I COULD COME **DIRECTLY.**

CHINK-ERR-CHING!

FIRST, YOU SHOULD HAVE SOME NEW **CLOTHES** TO COME IN, AND THEY SHOULD **NOT** BE WORKING-CLOTHES.

SAY THIS DAY WEEK. YOU'LL WANT SOME MONEY. SHALL I LEAVE YOU **TWENTY GUINEAS?**

WELL, JOSEPH GARGERY? YOU LOOK DUMB-FOUNDERED? IT WAS UNDERSTOOD THAT YOU WANTED **NOTHING** FOR YOURSELF, **REMEMBER?**

IT **WERE** UNDERSTOOD; AND IT **ARE** UNDERSTOOD. AND IT EVER **WILL BE** SIMILAR ACCORDING.

BUT **WHAT IF** IT WAS IN MY INSTRUCTIONS TO MAKE YOU A PRESENT, AS **COMPENSATION** FOR THE LOSS OF HIS SERVICES?

PIP IS THAT HEARTY WELCOME TO GO FREE WITH HIS SERVICES, TO HONOUR AND FORTUN', AS **NO WORDS** CAN TELL HIM.

BUT IF YOU THINK AS **MONEY** CAN MAKE COMPENSATION TO ME FUR THE LOSS OF THE LITTLE CHILD – WHAT COME TO THE FORGE – AND **EVER THE BEST OF FRIENDS...**

JOE'S VOICE DIED AWAY, AND HIS BROAD CHEST **HEAVED.** I **BEGGED** HIM TO BE COMFORTED.

NOW, JOSEPH GARGERY, I WARN YOU THIS IS YOUR **LAST** CHANCE.

IF YOU MEAN TO TAKE A **PRESENT** THAT I HAVE IT IN CHARGE TO MAKE YOU, SPEAK OUT, AND YOU SHALL **HAVE** IT.

IF ON THE **CONTRARY** YOU MEAN TO SAY --

WHICH I **MEANTERSAY,** THAT IF YOU COME INTO MY PLACE BULL-BAITING AND **BADGERING** ME, COME OUT!

WHICH I **MEANTERSAY** AS SECH IF YOU'RE A MAN, COME ON!

I DREW JOE AWAY, AND HE IMMEDIATELY BECAME PLACABLE.

WELL, MR. PIP, I THINK THE SOONER YOU **LEAVE** HERE – AS YOU ARE TO BE A **GENTLEMAN** – THE **BETTER.**

LET IT STAND FOR THIS DAY **WEEK,** AND YOU SHALL RECEIVE MY PRINTED **ADDRESS** IN THE MEANTIME.

I THINK HE WOULD HAVE GONE ON, BUT FOR HIS SEEMING TO THINK JOE **DANGEROUS** AND GOING OFF.

SOMETHING CAME INTO MY HEAD WHICH INDUCED ME TO RUN **AFTER** HIM.

I BEG YOUR PARDON, MR. JAGGERS. I WISH TO KEEP TO YOUR **DIRECTIONS;** SO I THOUGHT I HAD BETTER ASK.

WOULD THERE BE ANY **OBJECTION** TO MY TAKING LEAVE OF ANY ONE I KNOW, ABOUT HERE, BEFORE I GO AWAY? I DON'T MEAN IN THE VILLAGE ONLY; BUT UP-TOWN?

NO – NO OBJECTION.

THANK YOU, SIR.

I RAN HOME AGAIN.

JOE, HAVE YOU TOLD **BIDDY?**

NO, PIP. WHICH I LEFT IT TO YOURSELF, PIP.

I WOULD RATHER **YOU** TOLD, JOE.

THE NEXT MORNING, AFTER BREAKFAST, JOE BROUGHT OUT MY **INDENTURES** FROM THE PRESS IN THE BEST PARLOUR. WE PUT THEM IN THE **FIRE**, AND I FELT THAT I WAS **FREE**.

VOLUME I
CHAPTER XIX

AFTER CHURCH, AND AN EARLY DINNER, I STROLLED OUT **ALONE**.

AS I PASSED THE CHURCH, I THOUGHT, WITH SOMETHING ALLIED TO **SHAME**, OF MY COMPANIONSHIP WITH THE **FUGITIVE** WHOM I HAD ONCE SEEN LIMPING AMONG THOSE GRAVES. MY COMFORT WAS, THAT IT HAPPENED A **LONG** TIME AGO, AND THAT HE HAD DOUBTLESS BEEN TRANSPORTED A LONG WAY OFF, AND WAS **DEAD** TO ME.

I MADE MY **EXULTANT** WAY TO THE OLD BATTERY; AND, LYING DOWN THERE TO CONSIDER THE QUESTION WHETHER MISS HAVISHAM **INTENDED** ME FOR **ESTELLA**, FELL ASLEEP.

WHEN I AWOKE, I WAS MUCH **SURPRISED** TO FIND JOE SITTING BESIDE ME.

AS BEING THE **LAST** TIME, PIP, I THOUGHT I'D **FOLLER**.

I'M VERY **GLAD** YOU DID SO. YOU KNOW, I'D **ALWAYS** WANTED TO BE A GENTLEMAN.

HAVE YOU THOUGH? **ASTONISHING!**

IT'S A PITY NOW, JOE, THAT YOU DID NOT GET ON A LITTLE **MORE** WHEN WE HAD OUR **LESSONS** HERE; ISN'T IT?

WELL, I DON'T KNOW. I'M SO AWFUL **DULL**. I'M ONLY MASTER OF MY OWN TRADE. IT WERE ALWAYS A **PITY** AS I WAS SO AWFUL DULL.

MISS HAVISHAM MADE HER CRUTCH STICK PLAY ROUND ME, AS IF SHE WERE A **FAIRY GODMOTHER** WHO HAD **CHANGED** ME.

I HAVE COME INTO **SUCH** GOOD **FORTUNE** SINCE I SAW YOU LAST, MISS HAVISHAM. AND I AM SO **GRATEFUL** FOR IT, MISS HAVISHAM!

I HAVE SEEN MR. JAGGERS. I HAVE **HEARD** ABOUT IT, PIP.

WELL! YOU HAVE A **PROMISING** CAREER BEFORE YOU. BE GOOD - **DESERVE** IT - ABIDE BY MR. JAGGERS'S INSTRUCTIONS.

GOOD-BY, PIP! - YOU WILL **ALWAYS** KEEP THE NAME OF PIP, YOU KNOW.

ON THIS LAST EVENING, I DRESSED MYSELF OUT IN MY NEW CLOTHES FOR JOE AND BIDDY, AND SAT IN MY SPLENDOUR UNTIL BEDTIME. WE HAD A HOT SUPPER ON THE OCCASION. WE WERE ALL VERY **LOW**, AND NONE THE HIGHER FOR **PRETENDING** TO BE IN SPIRITS.

I WAS TO **LEAVE** OUR VILLAGE AT FIVE IN THE MORNING, AND HAD TOLD JOE THAT I WISHED TO WALK AWAY **ALONE**.

AFTER A HURRIED BREAKFAST, I TOOK UP MY LITTLE PORTMANTEAU AND WALKED OUT.

HOOROAR!

I WALKED AWAY AT A GOOD PACE, THINKING IT WAS **EASIER** TO GO THAN I HAD SUPPOSED.

BUT THE VILLAGE WAS VERY **PEACEFUL**, AND I HAD BEEN SO INNOCENT AND LITTLE THERE, AND ALL BEYOND WAS SO UNKNOWN AND GREAT, THAT IN A MOMENT I BROKE INTO **TEARS**.

I WAS BETTER AFTER I HAD CRIED - MORE SORRY, MORE **AWARE** OF MY OWN **INGRATITUDE**.

IT WAS NOW TOO **FAR** TO GO BACK. THE MISTS HAD ALL SOLEMNLY RISEN NOW...

...AND THE WORLD LAY SPREAD **BEFORE** ME.

**VOLUME II
CHAPTER I**

THE JOURNEY FROM OUR TOWN TO THE METROPOLIS WAS OF ABOUT FIVE HOURS. IT WAS A LITTLE PAST MIDDAY WHEN THE STAGE REACHED *CHEAPSIDE*, LONDON.

I WAS SCARED BY THE *IMMENSITY OF LONDON*. I THINK I MIGHT HAVE HAD SOME FAINT DOUBTS WHETHER IT WAS NOT RATHER *UGLY*, CROOKED, NARROW, AND *DIRTY*.

MR. JAGGERS HAD SENT ME HIS ADDRESS; IT WAS **LITTLE BRITAIN**, AND HE HAD WRITTEN AFTER IT ON HIS CARD, "JUST OUT OF SMITHFIELD, CLOSE BY THE COACH-OFFICE." A HACKNEY-COACHMAN PACKED ME UP IN HIS COACH, WHICH SOON STOPPED IN A **GLOOMY** STREET.

IS MR. JAGGERS AT HOME?

HE IS **NOT**. HE IS IN **COURT** AT PRESENT.

AM I ADDRESSING MR. PIP?

YES.

MR. JAGGERS LEFT WORD, WOULD YOU **WAIT** IN HIS ROOM? HE COULDN'T SAY HOW **LONG** HE MIGHT BE, HAVING A CASE ON. BUT HIS TIME BEING **VALUABLE**, THAT HE WON'T BE LONGER THAN HE CAN HELP.

MR. JAGGERS'S ROOM WAS A MOST **DISMAL** PLACE. THERE WERE TWO DREADFUL CASTS, OF FACES PECULIARLY **SWOLLEN**. I WONDERED WHETHER THEY WERE OF MR. JAGGERS'S **FAMILY**.

I SAT **WAITING**, UNTIL I REALLY COULD NOT **BEAR** THE TWO CASTS. I GOT UP AND TOLD THE CLERK THAT I WOULD TAKE A TURN IN THE AIR.

I TURNED INTO A STREET WHERE I SAW THE GREAT DOME OF SAINT PAUL'S BULGING FROM BEHIND A GRIM STONE BUILDING WHICH A BYSTANDER SAID WAS **NEWGATE PRISON**.

I SAW THE YARD WHERE THE **GALLOWS** WAS KEPT, AND WHERE PEOPLE WERE PUBLICLY WHIPPED. FOUR CONVICTS WERE TO COME OUT OF DEBTORS' DOOR TO BE **HANGED** THE DAY AFTER TOMORROW.

THIS GAVE ME A **SICKENING** IDEA OF LONDON.

RETURNING TO LITTLE BRITAIN, I BECAME AWARE THAT OTHER PEOPLE WERE WAITING ABOUT FOR MR. JAGGERS, AS WELL AS I. AT LENGTH I SAW MR. JAGGERS COMING ACROSS THE ROAD TOWARDS ME.

JAGGERS & CO

ALL THE OTHERS WHO WERE WAITING SAW HIM AT THE SAME TIME, AND THERE WAS QUITE A RUSH AT HIM.

NOW, I HAVE NOTHING TO SAY TO YOU. I WANT TO KNOW NO MORE THAN I KNOW.

AS TO THE RESULT, I TOLD YOU FROM THE FIRST IT WAS A TOSS-UP. HAVE YOU PAID WEMMICK?

YES, SIR.

WHAT ABOUT MY BILL, SIR?

NOW, I TELL YOU ONCE FOR ALL. IF YOU DON'T KNOW THAT YOUR BILL'S IN GOOD HANDS, I KNOW IT.

IF YOU COME HERE BOTHERING ME, I'LL MAKE AN EXAMPLE OF BOTH YOUR BILL AND YOU, AND LET HIM SLIP THROUGH MY FINGERS. HAVE YOU PAID WEMMICK?

OH YES, SIR! EVERY FARDEN.

MY GUARDIAN TOOK ME INTO HIS ROOM. WHILE HE LUNCHED, HE INFORMED ME WHAT ARRANGEMENTS HE HAD MADE FOR ME.

I WAS TO GO TO "BARNARD'S INN"; TO YOUNG MR. POCKET'S ROOMS; I WAS TO REMAIN WITH YOUNG MR. POCKET UNTIL MONDAY, AND THEN GO WITH HIM TO HIS FATHER'S HOUSE; THAT I MIGHT TRY HOW I LIKED IT.

I WAS TOLD WHAT MY ALLOWANCE WAS TO BE – IT WAS VERY LIBERAL – AND HANDED THE CARDS OF TRADESMEN.

YOU WILL FIND YOUR CREDIT GOOD, MR. PIP, BUT I SHALL BY THIS MEANS BE ABLE TO CHECK YOUR BILLS, AND PULL YOU UP IF I FIND YOU OUTRUNNING THE CONSTABLE.

OF COURSE YOU'LL GO WRONG SOMEHOW, BUT THAT'S NO FAULT OF MINE.

I THEN FOUND THAT WEMMICK, THE CLERK, SHOULD WALK ROUND WITH ME.

I TELL YOU IT'S NO USE; HE WON'T HAVE A WORD TO SAY TO ONE OF YOU.

VOLUME II
CHAPTER II

WE SOON GOT **CLEAR** OF THE CROWD, AND WENT ON SIDE BY SIDE.

SO YOU WERE **NEVER** IN LONDON BEFORE? I WAS NEW HERE **ONCE**. RUM TO THINK OF **NOW**!

IS IT A **VERY** WICKED PLACE?

YOU MAY GET **CHEATED, ROBBED,** AND **MURDERED** IN LONDON. BUT THERE ARE PLENTY OF PEOPLE **ANYWHERE,** WHO'LL DO **THAT** FOR YOU.

EVENTUALLY MR. WEMMICK SAID WE WERE AT BARNARD'S INN.

I HAD **SUPPOSED** THAT ESTABLISHMENT TO BE AN HOTEL KEPT BY MR. BARNARD, BUT I NOW FOUND BARNARD TO BE A DISEMBODIED SPIRIT, AND HIS INN THE **DINGIEST** COLLECTION OF SHABBY BUILDINGS EVER **SQUEEZED** TOGETHER IN A **RANK** CORNER.

HE LED ME UP A FLIGHT OF STAIRS, WHICH APPEARED TO BE SLOWLY **COLLAPSING** INTO SAWDUST, TO A SET OF CHAMBERS ON THE TOP FLOOR.

HE HARDLY THOUGHT YOU'D COME SO **SOON.** YOU DON'T WANT ME ANY MORE?

NO, THANK YOU.

Return SHORTLY

AS I KEEP THE **CASH,** WE SHALL MOST LIKELY MEET PRETTY OFTEN. GOOD DAY.

MR. POCKET, JUNIOR'S, IDEA OF SHORTLY WAS NOT **MINE,** FOR I HAD NEARLY MADDENED MYSELF WITH LOOKING AT THE GRIMY VIEW FOR HALF AN HOUR, BEFORE I HEARD FOOTSTEPS ON THE STAIRS.

MR. PIP? DEAR ME! I AM EXTREMELY **SORRY.** I KNEW THERE WAS A COACH FROM YOUR PART OF THE COUNTRY AT MIDDAY.

THE FACT IS, I HAVE BEEN OUT ON **YOUR** ACCOUNT, FOR I THOUGHT, COMING FROM THE COUNTRY, YOU MIGHT LIKE A LITTLE FRUIT AFTER DINNER.

AS I STOOD OPPOSITE TO MR. POCKET, JUNIOR, I SAW THE STARTING APPEARANCE COME INTO HIS **OWN** EYES THAT I **KNEW** TO BE IN MINE.

LORD BLESS ME, **YOU'RE** THE PROWLING BOY!

AND **YOU** ARE THE PALE YOUNG GENTLEMAN!

VOLUME II
CHAPTER III

THE IDEA OF ITS BEING **YOU!**

THE IDEA OF ITS BEING YOU! – WELL! IT'S ALL OVER NOW, I HOPE, AND IT WILL BE **MAGNANIMOUS** IN YOU IF YOU'LL **FORGIVE** ME FOR HAVING KNOCKED YOU ABOUT SO.

I DERIVED FROM THIS SPEECH THAT MR. HERBERT POCKET STILL RATHER CONFOUNDED HIS **INTENTION** WITH HIS **EXECUTION.**

MISS HAVISHAM HAD SENT FOR ME ON A **TRIAL** VISIT, AND IF I HAD COME OUT OF IT SUCCESSFULLY, I SUPPOSE I SHOULD HAVE BEEN **PROVIDED** FOR –

PERHAPS I SHOULD HAVE BEEN WHAT-YOU-MAY-CALLED IT TO ESTELLA – BETROTHED. **ENGAGED.**

HOW DID YOU BEAR YOUR DISAPPOINTMENT?

POOH! SHE'S A **TARTAR.**

MISS HAVISHAM?

I MEANT **ESTELLA.** THAT GIRL'S **HARD** AND **HAUGHTY** AND **CAPRICIOUS** TO THE LAST DEGREE. SHE HAS BEEN BROUGHT UP BY MISS HAVISHAM TO WREAK **REVENGE** ON ALL THE MALE SEX.

WHAT RELATION IS SHE TO MISS HAVISHAM?

NONE, ONLY **ADOPTED.**

WHY **SHOULD** SHE WREAK REVENGE?

LORD, MR. PIP! DON'T YOU **KNOW?** DEAR ME! IT'S QUITE A STORY, AND SHALL BE SAVED TILL DINNER-TIME.

MR. JAGGERS IS YOUR **GUARDIAN,** I UNDERSTAND? YOU KNOW HE IS MISS HAVISHAM'S **SOLICITOR,** AND HAS HER CONFIDENCE WHEN NOBODY ELSE HAS?

HE WAS SO OBLIGING AS TO SUGGEST MY **FATHER** FOR YOUR TUTOR. MY FATHER IS MISS HAVISHAM'S COUSIN; NOT THAT THAT IMPLIES FAMILIAR INTERCOURSE BETWEEN THEM, FOR HE IS A **BAD** COURTIER AND WILL NOT PROPITIATE HER.

AS HE WAS SO COMMUNICATIVE, I TOLD HIM MY SMALL STORY; AND LAID STRESS ON MY BEING **FORBIDDEN** TO INQUIRE WHO MY BENEFACTOR WAS.

AS I HAVE BEEN BROUGHT UP A BLACKSMITH IN A COUNTRY PLACE, AND KNOW VERY LITTLE OF THE WAYS OF **POLITENESS**, I WOULD TAKE IT AS A KINDNESS IF YOU WOULD GIVE ME A HINT WHENEVER YOU SEE ME GOING WRONG.

WITH **PLEASURE**.

WILL YOU DO ME THE FAVOUR TO CALL ME BY MY CHRISTIAN NAME, HERBERT?

THANK YOU. MY CHRISTIAN NAME IS PHILIP.

I DON'T **TAKE** TO PHILIP. I TELL YOU WHAT I SHOULD LIKE – WE ARE SO **HARMONIOUS**, AND YOU HAVE BEEN A BLACKSMITH – WOULD YOU MIND **HANDEL** FOR A FAMILIAR NAME?

THERE'S A **CHARMING** PIECE OF MUSIC BY HANDEL, CALLED *THE HARMONIOUS BLACKSMITH*.

I SHOULD LIKE IT **VERY** MUCH.

THEN, MY DEAR **HANDEL**, HERE IS THE DINNER. I MUST BEG OF YOU TO TAKE THE **TOP** OF THE TABLE, BECAUSE THE DINNER IS OF **YOUR** PROVIDING.

THIS I WOULD NOT HEAR OF, SO HE TOOK THE TOP. WE HAD MADE SOME PROGRESS IN THE DINNER, WHEN I REMINDED HIM OF HIS **PROMISE** TO TELL ME ABOUT MISS HAVISHAM.

MISS HAVISHAM, YOU MUST KNOW, WAS A **SPOILT** CHILD. HER MOTHER **DIED** WHEN SHE WAS A BABY, AND HER FATHER DENIED HER **NOTHING**.

HER FATHER WAS A COUNTRY GENTLEMAN DOWN IN **YOUR** PART OF THE WORLD; AND WAS A BREWER.

MR. HAVISHAM WAS VERY **RICH** AND VERY **PROUD**. SO WAS HIS **DAUGHTER**.

MISS HAVISHAM WAS AN **ONLY** CHILD?

NO, SHE HAD A **HALF-BROTHER**. HER FATHER PRIVATELY MARRIED AGAIN – HIS **COOK**, I RATHER THINK. IN THE COURSE OF TIME SHE DIED, AND THEN THE SON BECAME A PART OF THE **FAMILY**.

AS HE GREW UP, HE TURNED OUT RIOTOUS AND UNDUTIFUL. HIS FATHER **DISINHERITED** HIM, BUT LATER **SOFTENED**, AND LEFT HIM WELL OFF, THOUGH NOT NEARLY SO WELL OFF AS MISS HAVISHAM.

SHE WAS NOW AN **HEIRESS**, AND LOOKED AFTER AS A GREAT MATCH.

HER HALF-BROTHER **WASTED** HIS AMPLE MEANS. THERE WERE STRONG DIFFERENCES BETWEEN THEM, AND IT IS SUSPECTED THAT HE CHERISHED A DEEP **GRUDGE** AGAINST HER.

THERE **APPEARED** UPON THE SCENE – SAY AT THE RACES OR THE PUBLIC BALLS, OR ANYWHERE ELSE YOU LIKE – A CERTAIN **MAN**, WHO MADE **LOVE** TO MISS HAVISHAM. ALL THIS HAPPENED FIVE-AND-TWENTY YEARS AGO. HE WAS A **SHOWY** MAN.

MY FATHER **WARNED** HER THAT SHE WAS DOING **TOO MUCH** FOR THIS MAN, AND WAS PLACING HERSELF TOO UNRESERVEDLY IN HIS POWER.

HE **PURSUED** MISS HAVISHAM, AND PROFESSED TO BE **DEVOTED** TO HER. AND SHE FELL PASSIONATELY IN **LOVE** WITH HIM. HE PRACTISED ON HER AFFECTION, AND GOT GREAT SUMS OF **MONEY** FROM HER.

SHE TOOK THE FIRST OPPORTUNITY OF **ANGRILY** ORDERING MY FATHER **OUT** OF THE HOUSE, AND MY FATHER HAS NEVER SEEN HER **SINCE**.

SHE WAS TOO **HAUGHTY** AND TOO MUCH IN **LOVE** TO BE **ADVISED** BY ANYONE.

THE **MARRIAGE DAY** WAS FIXED, THE WEDDING **DRESSES** WERE BOUGHT, THE WEDDING **TOUR** WAS PLANNED OUT, THE WEDDING **GUESTS** WERE INVITED.

THE **DAY** CAME, BUT **NOT** THE BRIDEGROOM. HE WROTE HER A **LETTER** --

WHICH SHE RECEIVED WHEN SHE WAS **DRESSING**? AT TWENTY MINUTES TO NINE?

THE HOUR AND MINUTE AT WHICH SHE AFTERWARDS **STOPPED** THE CLOCKS.

THE LETTER **HEARTLESSLY** BROKE THE MARRIAGE OFF.

WHEN SHE RECOVERED FROM A BAD ILLNESS, SHE LAID THE WHOLE PLACE **WASTE**, AND HAS NEVER SINCE LOOKED UPON THE LIGHT OF DAY. BUT I HAVE **FORGOTTEN** ONE THING.

IT IS SUPPOSED THAT THE MAN TO WHOM SHE GAVE HER CONFIDENCE ACTED THROUGHOUT IN **CONCERT** WITH HER HALF-BROTHER, AND THAT THEY **SHARED** THE PROFITS.

WHAT **BECAME** OF THE TWO MEN?

THEY FELL INTO **DEEPER** SHAME AND RUIN. I DON'T KNOW IF THEY ARE STILL **ALIVE** TODAY.

WE PASSED ON TO **OTHER** SUBJECTS. I LEARNED THAT MY FRIEND HAD GREAT **PLANS** FOR **TRADING** WITH THE EAST AND WEST INDIES, BUT WAS PRESENTLY EMPLOYED IN A COUNTING-HOUSE.

BUT THE THING IS THAT YOU LOOK ABOUT YOU. **THEN** THE TIME COMES WHEN YOU SEE YOUR **OPENING**. AND YOU GO IN AND YOU **SWOOP** UPON IT AND YOU MAKE YOUR **CAPITAL**, AND THEN **THERE** YOU ARE!

WHEN YOU HAVE ONCE MADE YOUR CAPITAL, YOU HAVE **NOTHING** TO DO BUT **EMPLOY** IT.

IN THE COMPANY OF ONE WHO HAD **ALREADY** MADE HIS FORTUNE IN HIS OWN **MIND**, IT SEEMED MANY MONTHS SINCE I HAD LEFT JOE AND BIDDY.

ON THE MONDAY MORNING, HERBERT WENT TO THE COUNTING-HOUSE TO **LOOK ABOUT** HIM, AND I BORE HIM COMPANY.

AFTER LUNCH, WE TOOK COACH FOR **HAMMERSMITH**, WHERE MR. MATTHEW POCKET LIVED. WE WALKED TO HIS HOUSE AND WE PASSED DIRECT INTO A LITTLE GARDEN OVERLOOKING THE RIVER, WHERE MR. POCKET'S **CHILDREN** WERE PLAYING ABOUT.

MR. POCKET CAME OUT TO MAKE MY ACQUAINTANCE.

BELINDA, I HOPE YOU HAVE **WELCOMED** MR. PIP?

YES...

MRS. POCKET WAS THE DAUGHTER OF A **KNIGHT**, WHO HAD DIRECTED THAT SHE BE BROUGHT UP TO MARRY A TITLE – HIGHLY **ORNAMENTAL**, BUT PERFECTLY **USELESS**.

WITH HER CHARACTER THUS FORMED, IN THE FIRST BLOOM OF HER YOUTH SHE HAD ENCOUNTERED THE **UNTITLED** MR. POCKFT, AND HAD **MARRIED** HIM WITHOUT THE KNOWLEDGE OF THE **PARENT**.

MR. POCKET TOOK ME INTO THE HOUSE AND SHOWED ME MY ROOM, WHICH WAS A **PLEASANT** ONE. HE THEN KNOCKED AT THE DOORS OF TWO OTHER SIMILAR ROOMS, AND INTRODUCED ME TO THEIR OCCUPANTS, BY NAME **DRUMMLE** AND **STARTOP**.

BOTH MR. AND MRS. POCKET HAD SUCH A NOTICEABLE AIR OF BEING IN SOMEBODY ELSE'S **HANDS**, THAT I WONDERED WHO **REALLY** WAS IN POSSESSION OF THE HOUSE AND LET THEM LIVE THERE. AT DINNER I FOUND THIS UNKNOWN POWER TO BE THE **SERVANTS**.

MR. AND MRS. POCKET HAD A **TOADY** NEIGHBOUR; A WIDOW LADY WHO AGREED WITH EVERYBODY ACCORDING TO CIRCUMSTANCES. THIS LADY'S NAME WAS MRS. COILER, AND I HAD THE **HONOUR** OF TAKING HER DOWN TO DINNER.

THE PAGE CAME IN WITH THE ANNOUNCEMENT OF A DOMESTIC AFFLICTION: THE COOK HAD MISLAID THE BEEF. TO MY **AMAZEMENT**, I SAW MR. POCKET RELIEVE HIS MIND THROUGH AN **EXTRAORDINARY** PERFORMANCE. HE PUT HIS HANDS INTO HIS DISTURBED HAIR, AND APPEARED TO TRY TO **LIFT** HIMSELF UP BY IT.

HIS PERFORMANCE MADE **NO** IMPRESSION ON ANYBODY ELSE, AND I SOON BECAME AS **FAMILIAR** WITH IT AS THE REST.

AFTER DINNER, AND A ROW ON THE RIVER, I THINK WE **SHOULD** ALL HAVE ENJOYED OURSELVES, BUT FOR A RATHER **DISAGREEABLE** DOMESTIC OCCURRENCE. THE COOK WAS LYING **DRUNK** ON THE KITCHEN FLOOR.

AM I, GRANDPAPA'S GRANDDAUGHTER, TO BE **NOTHING** IN THE HOUSE? BESIDES, THE COOK HAS SAID THAT SHE FELT I WAS BORN TO BE A **DUCHESS**.

GOOD NIGHT, MR. PIP!!!

AFTER TWO OR THREE DAYS, MR. POCKET AND I HAD A LONG TALK. MR. JAGGERS HAD TOLD HIM THAT I WAS NOT DESIGNED FOR ANY **PROFESSION**; AND THAT I SHOULD BE WELL ENOUGH EDUCATED IF I COULD "HOLD MY OWN" WITH THE **AVERAGE** YOUNG MAN IN **PROSPEROUS** CIRCUMSTANCES.

HE **ADVISED** MY ATTENDING CERTAIN PLACES IN LONDON FOR THE ACQUISITION OF CERTAIN RUDIMENTS. HE WOULD ACT AS EXPLAINER AND DIRECTOR OF ALL MY **STUDIES**.

IT OCCURRED TO ME THAT IF I COULD **RETAIN** MY BEDROOM IN BARNARD'S INN, MY LIFE WOULD BE AGREEABLY VARIED, WHILE MY MANNERS WOULD BE **NONE** THE **WORSE** FOR HERBERT'S SOCIETY. MR. POCKET DID NOT OBJECT TO THIS ARRANGEMENT, BUT **URGED** THAT IT MUST BE SUBMITTED TO MY **GUARDIAN**.

I THEREFORE WENT TO LITTLE BRITAIN AND IMPARTED MY **WISH** TO MR. JAGGERS.

IF I COULD **BUY** THE FURNITURE NOW HIRED FOR ME, AND ONE OR TWO **OTHER** LITTLE THINGS, I SHOULD BE QUITE AT **HOME** THERE.

GO IT! I TOLD YOU YOU'D GET ON. WELL! HOW **MUCH** MONEY DO YOU **WANT**?

HOW MUCH? **FIFTY** POUNDS?

OH, NOT **NEARLY** SO MUCH.

FIVE POUNDS?

OH, MORE THAN **THAT**.

MORE THAN THAT, EH? COME! LET'S GET AT IT.

TWICE FIVE; WILL THAT DO? **FOUR** TIMES FIVE; WILL **THAT** DO?

I THINK THAT WILL DO HANDSOMELY.

WEMMICK! TAKE MR. PIP'S WRITTEN ORDER, AND PAY HIM TWENTY POUNDS.

MR. JAGGERS HAPPENED TO GO **OUT** AND WEMMICK WAS BRISK AND TALKATIVE.

I HARDLY KNOW WHAT TO **MAKE** OF MR. JAGGERS'S MANNER.

TELL HIM THAT, AND HE'LL TAKE IT AS A **COMPLIMENT**. HE DON'T MEAN THAT YOU SHOULD KNOW WHAT TO MAKE OF IT.

OH – IT'S NOT PERSONAL; IT'S **PROFESSIONAL**. ALWAYS SEEMS TO ME, AS IF HE HAD SET A **MAN-TRAP** AND WAS WATCHING IT.

SUDDENLY – CLICK – YOU'RE CAUGHT!

PRAY, WHOSE *LIKENESSES* ARE THOSE?

THESE? THESE ARE TWO *CELEBRATED* ONES. FAMOUS CLIENTS THAT GOT US A WORLD OF CREDIT.

THIS CHAP MURDERED HIS MASTER. THE CAST WAS MADE IN *NEWGATE*, DIRECTLY AFTER HE WAS TAKEN *DOWN*.

YOU HAD A *PARTICULAR* FANCY FOR ME, HADN'T YOU, OLD ARTFUL? HAD IT MADE FOR ME, EXPRESS!

DID THAT OTHER CREATURE COME TO THE *SAME* END? HE HAS THE SAME *LOOK*.

YES, HE CAME TO THE SAME END. HE FORGED *WILLS*, THIS BLADE DID, IF HE DIDN'T ALSO PUT THE SUPPOSED TESTATORS TO *SLEEP* TOO. HE SENT OUT TO *BUY* THIS FOR ME, ONLY THE DAY BEFORE.

ARE ALL YOUR PERSONAL JEWELLERY DERIVED FROM *LIKE* SOURCES?

OH YES, THESE ARE *ALL* GIFTS OF *THAT* KIND. ONE BRINGS ANOTHER, THAT'S THE WAY OF IT. I ALWAYS TAKE 'EM.

AFTER ALL, THEY'RE *PROPERTY* AND *PORTABLE*.

MY GUIDING-STAR ALWAYS IS, "GET HOLD OF *PORTABLE PROPERTY*".

IF AT ANY TIME WHEN YOU HAVE NOTHING *BETTER* TO DO, AND WOULDN'T MIND COMING OVER TO SEE ME AT WALWORTH, I COULD OFFER YOU A BED, AND CONSIDER IT AN *HONOUR*.

I HAVE TWO OR THREE *CURIOSITIES* YOU MIGHT LIKE TO LOOK OVER.

I SHOULD BE *DELIGHTED* TO ACCEPT YOUR *HOSPITALITY*.

HAVE YOU *DINED* WITH MR. JAGGERS YET?

NOT YET.

WHEN YOU *DO*, LOOK AT HIS *HOUSEKEEPER*. YOU'LL SEE A WILD BEAST TAMED. KEEP YOUR EYE ON IT.

67

IT FELL OUT AS WEMMICK HAD **TOLD** ME IT WOULD, THAT I HAD AN EARLY OPPORTUNITY OF COMPARING MY **GUARDIAN'S** ESTABLISHMENT WITH THAT OF HIS CASHIER AND CLERK.

VOLUME II
CHAPTER VII

MY GUARDIAN GAVE ME AN **INVITATION** FOR MYSELF AND FRIENDS FOR DINNER AT HIS ESTABLISHMENT.

THE **HOUSEKEEPER** APPEARED WITH THE FIRST DISH FOR THE TABLE.

OUR CONVERSATION TURNED UPON OUR **ROWING** FEATS. DRUMMLE WAS RALLIED FOR COMING UP BEHIND IN HIS SLOW AMPHIBIOUS WAY. UPON THIS, DRUMMLE INFORMED OUR HOST THAT AS TO STRENGTH, HE COULD SCATTER US LIKE **CHAFF**. THE **SPIDER**, AS MR. JAGGERS CALLED HIM, FELL TO BARING HIS ARM TO SHOW HOW **MUSCULAR** IT WAS, AND WE ALL FELL TO BARING OUR ARMS IN A RIDICULOUS MANNER.

THE HOUSEKEEPER WAS AT THAT TIME **CLEARING** THE TABLE. MY GUARDIAN SUDDENLY CLAPPED HIS LARGE HAND ON THE HOUSEKEEPER'S, LIKE A **TRAP**, AS SHE STRETCHED IT ACROSS THE TABLE.

IF YOU TALK OF STRENGTH, I'LL **SHOW** YOU A WRIST. MOLLY; LET THEM SEE YOUR **WRIST**.

Master, *don't*.

MOLLY; LET THEM SEE **BOTH** YOUR WRISTS. **SHOW** THEM. COME!

THERE'S **POWER** HERE. VERY FEW MEN HAVE THE POWER OF WRIST THAT THIS WOMAN HAS.

IT'S **REMARKABLE** WHAT FORCE OF **GRIP** THERE IS IN THESE HANDS.

THAT'LL DO, MOLLY. YOU HAVE BEEN **ADMIRED**, AND CAN GO.

AT HALF-PAST NINE, GENTLEMEN, WE MUST BREAK UP. PRAY MAKE THE BEST USE OF YOUR TIME.

AND AT HALF-PAST NINE WE DEPARTED.

A MONTH OR SO LATER, I RECEIVED A LETTER BY THE POST.

My dear Mr. Pip:

I write this by request of Mr. Gargery, for to let you know that he is going to London, and would be glad if agreeable to be allowed to see you. He would call at Barnard's Hotel Tuesday morning 9 o'clock.

Your poor sister is much the same as when you left. We talk of you in the kitchen every night, and wonder what you are doing. No more, dear Mr. Pip, from your ever obliged and affectionate servant,

Biddy.

P.S. he wishes me most particular to write what larks.

THE APPOINTMENT WAS FOR **NEXT DAY**.

LET ME CONFESS **EXACTLY** WITH WHAT FEELINGS I LOOKED FORWARD TO JOE'S COMING. NOT WITH PLEASURE, THOUGH I WAS BOUND TO HIM BY SO MANY TIES – NO, WITH CONSIDERABLE DISTURBANCE, **MORTIFICATION**, AND A KEEN SENSE OF **INCONGRUITY**.

IF I COULD HAVE KEPT HIM **AWAY** BY PAYING MONEY, I CERTAINLY WOULD HAVE **PAID** MONEY.

I GOT UP **EARLY** IN THE MORNING, AND CAUSED OUR ROOMS IN BARNARD'S INN TO ASSUME THEIR MOST **SPLENDID** APPEARANCE. AS THE TIME APPROACHED I SHOULD HAVE LIKED TO **RUN AWAY**, BUT PRESENTLY I HEARD JOE ON THE STAIRCASE.

I **KNEW** IT WAS JOE BY HIS **CLUMSY** MANNER OF COMING UP STAIRS. AT LAST HE STOPPED OUTSIDE OUR DOOR, AND GAVE A FAINT SINGLE RAP.

≋tap≋

JOE, HOW ARE YOU, JOE?

PIP, HOW **AIR** YOU, PIP?

I AM GLAD TO **SEE** YOU, JOE.

WHICH YOU HAVE THAT GROWED, AND THAT SWELLED, AND THAT – GENTLE-FOLKED – AS TO BE SURE YOU ARE A **HONOUR** TO YOUR KING AND COUNTRY.

AND YOU, JOE, LOOK **WONDERFULLY** WELL.

US TWO BEING **ALONE**, SIR...

JOE, **HOW** CAN YOU CALL **ME**, SIR?

US TWO BEING **ALONE**, AND ME HAVING THE INTENTION TO STAY NOT MANY MINUTES **MORE**, I WILL NOW MENTION WHAT HAVE **LED** TO MY HAVING THE PRESENT **HONOUR**.

WELL, SIR, I WERE AT THE BARGEMEN T'OTHER NIGHT, WHEN THERE COME UP, **PUMBLECHOOK**, WHICH HIS MANNERS IS GIVEN TO BLUSTEROUS, PIP, AND HIS WORD WERE, "JOSEPH, MISS HAVISHAM SHE WISH TO SPEAK TO YOU."

NEXT DAY, **SIR**, HAVING **CLEANED** MYSELF, I GO AND I SEE MISS A.

MISS A., JOE? MISS HAVISHAM?

WHICH I **SAY**, SIR – MISS A., OR OTHERWAYS HAVISHAM. HER EXPRESSION AIR THEN AS FOLLERING: "MR. GARGERY. YOU AIR IN CORRESPONDENCE WITH MR. PIP? WOULD YOU TELL HIM, THAT **ESTELLA** HAS COME **HOME** AND WOULD BE GLAD TO SEE HIM."

I HAVE NOW **CONCLUDED**, SIR, AND, PIP, I WISH YOU EVER WELL AND EVER **PROSPERING** TO A GREATER AND A GREATER **HEIGHT**.

BUT YOU ARE NOT GOING **NOW**, JOE?

YES I AM.

PIP, DEAR OLD CHAP, LIFE IS MADE OF EVER SO MANY PARTINGS WELDED **TOGETHER**. IF THERE'S BEEN ANY FAULT AT ALL TODAY, IT'S **MINE**. YOU AND ME IS NOT TWO FIGURES TO BE TOGETHER IN LONDON; NOR YET ANYWHERES **ELSE** BUT WHAT IS **PRIVATE**.

IT AIN'T THAT I AM **PROUD**, BUT THAT I WANT TO BE **RIGHT**. I'M WRONG IN THESE CLOTHES. I'M WRONG OUT OF THE FORGE, THE KITCHEN; OR OFF TH' MESHES. AND SO GOD **BLESS** YOU, DEAR OLD PIP, OLD CHAP, **GOD BLESS YOU!**

HE TOUCHED ME **GENTLY** ON THE FOREHEAD AND WENT OUT.

IT WAS **CLEAR** THAT I MUST REPAIR TO OUR TOWN NEXT DAY; AND I SECURED MY BOX-PLACE BY TOMORROW'S AFTERNOON COACH.

IN THE FIRST FLOW OF MY **REPENTANCE**, IT WAS EQUALLY CLEAR THAT I MUST **STAY AT JOE'S**. BUT LATER, I BEGAN TO **INVENT** REASONS AND MAKE **EXCUSES** FOR PUTTING UP AT THE BLUE BOAR.

NEXT DAY, I ARRIVED ON THE GROUND WITH A QUARTER OF AN HOUR TO SPARE. AT THAT TIME, IT WAS CUSTOMARY TO CARRY **CONVICTS** DOWN TO THE DOCKYARDS BY STAGE-COACH.

AS I HAD OFTEN HEARD OF THEM IN THE CAPACITY OF **OUTSIDE** PASSENGERS, I WAS NOT SURPRISED WHEN I FOUND THERE WERE **TWO CONVICTS** GOING DOWN WITH ME.

YOU DON'T **MIND** THEM HANDEL?

OH NO! I DON'T MIND THEM.

SEE! THERE THEY ARE. WHAT A DEGRADED AND **VILE** SIGHT IT IS!

THE TWO CONVICTS WERE HANDCUFFED TOGETHER, AND HAD IRONS ON THEIR LEGS – IRONS OF A PATTERN I KNEW WELL. **ONE** WAS TALLER AND STOUTER THAN THE OTHER.

I **KNEW** HIS HALF-CLOSED EYE AT ONE GLANCE. **THERE** STOOD THE MAN WHO HAD SHOWED ME THE **FILE** AT **THE JOLLY BARGEMEN!**

THE WEATHER WAS MISERABLY **RAW**. IT MADE US ALL **LETHARGIC** BEFORE WE HAD GONE FAR.

I **DOZED OFF**, MYSELF, IN CONSIDERING THE QUESTION WHETHER I SHOULD **RESTORE** A COUPLE OF **POUNDS** STERLING TO THIS CREATURE BEFORE LOSING SIGHT OF HIM, AND HOW IT COULD **BEST** BE DONE.

73

BETIMES IN THE MORNING I WAS UP AND OUT. IT WAS TOO **EARLY** YET TO GO TO MISS HAVISHAM'S, SO I LOITERED INTO THE COUNTRY, THINKING ABOUT MY PATRONESS, AND PAINTING **BRILLIANT** PICTURES OF HER **PLANS** FOR ME.

VOLUME II
CHAPTER X

I SO SHAPED OUT MY WALK AS TO **ARRIVE** AT THE GATE AT MY OLD TIME. WHEN I HAD RUNG AT THE BELL WITH AN **UNSTEADY** HAND, I TURNED MY BACK UPON THE GATE.

SHE HAD **ADOPTED** ESTELLA, SHE HAD AS **GOOD** AS ADOPTED **ME**, AND IT COULD NOT **FAIL** TO BE HER **INTENTION** TO BRING US **TOGETHER**.

ORLICK!

AH, YOUNG MASTER, THERE'S **MORE** CHANGES THAN **YOURS**. BUT COME IN. IT'S OPPOSED TO MY ORDERS TO HOLD THE GATE OPEN.

THEN YOU HAVE **LEFT** THE FORGE?

DO THIS **LOOK** LIKE THE **FORGE**?

ORLICK SOUNDED A BELL, AND **LEFT** ME TO ASCEND THE STAIRCASE IN THE **DARK**. I TAPPED IN MY OLD WAY AT THE DOOR OF MISS HAVISHAM'S ROOM.

tap-ta-tap

PIP'S RAP. **COME IN**, PIP

SITTING **NEAR** HER WAS AN ELEGANT LADY WHOM I HAD **NEVER** SEEN.

COME IN, PIP, HOW DO YOU **DO**, PIP?

SO YOU KISS MY HAND AS IF I WERE A **QUEEN**, EH? – WELL?

I HEARD, MISS HAVISHAM, THAT YOU WERE SO **KIND** AS TO WISH ME TO COME AND **SEE** YOU, AND I CAME **DIRECTLY**.

WELL?

THE LADY WHOM I HAD **NEVER** SEEN BEFORE, LIFTED UP HER **EYES** AND LOOKED AT ME...

...AND THEN I SAW THAT THE EYES WERE **ESTELLA'S** EYES.

SHE WAS SO MUCH *CHANGED*, SO MUCH MORE *BEAUTIFUL*, SO MUCH MORE *WOMANLY*, THAT AS I LOOKED AT HER, I SLIPPED *HOPELESSLY* BACK INTO THE COARSE AND COMMON *BOY* AGAIN.

I -- IT'S A -- P-P-*PLEASURE* TO S-SEE YOU AGAIN. I'VE LOOKED F-FORWARD TO IT -- FOR -- A *LONG* T-TIME.

YOU FIND HER *MUCH* CHANGED, PIP?

WHEN I CAME IN, MISS HAVISHAM, I THOUGHT THERE WAS *NOTHING* OF ESTELLA IN THE FACE OR FIGURE;

BUT NOW IT ALL SETTLES DOWN SO *CURIOUSLY* INTO THE OLD...

WHAT? YOU ARE NOT GOING TO SAY INTO THE OLD ESTELLA? SHE WAS *PROUD* AND *INSULTING*. DON'T YOU *REMEMBER*?

THAT WAS *LONG* AGO, AND I KNEW NO *BETTER* THEN.

I HAVE NO DOUBT THAT YOU ARE QUITE *RIGHT*. I WAS VERY *DISAGREEABLE*.

WHEN WE HAD *CONVERSED* FOR A WHILE, MISS HAVISHAM SENT US TWO OUT TO WALK IN THE NEGLECTED GARDEN. I, *TREMBLING* IN SPIRIT AND WORSHIPPING THE VERY *HEM* OF HER DRESS; SHE, QUITE *COMPOSED* AND MOST DECIDEDLY *NOT* WORSHIPPING THE HEM OF *MINE*.

AS WE CAME *BACK* INTO THE YARD, I *SHOWED* HER WHERE SHE HAD GIVEN ME MY MEAT AND DRINK.

I DON'T REMEMBER.

NOT REMEMBER THAT YOU MADE ME *CRY*?

NO.

ESTELLA NOT REMEMBERING OR MINDING IN THE *LEAST*, MADE ME CRY *AGAIN*, INWARDLY.

YOU MUST KNOW, THAT I HAVE *NO HEART* – IF THAT HAS ANYTHING TO DO WITH MY MEMORY.

OH! I HAVE A *HEART* TO BE *STABBED* IN OR *SHOT* IN, I HAVE NO DOUBT. BUT YOU KNOW WHAT I *MEAN*.

I HAVE NO *SOFTNESS* THERE, NO – SYMPATHY, SENTIMENT – *NONSENSE*.

WHAT *WAS* IT THAT WAS BORNE IN UPON MY MIND WHEN SHE LOOKED ATTENTIVELY AT ME? ANYTHING THAT I HAD SEEN IN MISS HAVISHAM?

NO, IT WAS *NOT* MISS HAVISHAM. *WHO* THEN?

I LOOKED *AGAIN*, AND THE SUGGESTION WAS *GONE*.

AT LAST WE WENT BACK INTO THE HOUSE, AND THERE I HEARD, WITH SURPRISE, THAT MY *GUARDIAN* WAS THERE ON *BUSINESS* AND WOULD COME TO *DINNER.*

MISS HAVISHAM WAS IN HER CHAIR AND *WAITING* FOR ME. IT WAS LIKE PUSHING THE CHAIR ITSELF BACK INTO THE *PAST*, WHEN WE BEGAN THE OLD CIRCUIT ROUND ABOUT THE *ASHES* OF THE BRIDAL FEAST.

IS SHE BEAUTIFUL, GRACEFUL, WELL-GROWN?

DO YOU *ADMIRE* HER?

EVERYBODY *MUST* WHO *SEES* HER, MISS HAVISHAM.

LOVE HER, *LOVE HER,* LOVE HER!

IF SHE *FAVOURS* YOU, *LOVE* HER. IF SHE *WOUNDS* YOU, *LOVE* HER. IF SHE *TEARS* YOUR HEART TO *PIECES*, LOVE HER, *LOVE* HER!

HEAR ME, PIP! I ADOPTED HER, TO BE LOVED. I BRED HER AND EDUCATED HER, TO BE LOVED.

LOVE HER!

AAAEEEEEEEK!

AS I DREW HER DOWN AGAIN, I WAS CONSCIOUS OF A SCENT THAT I *KNEW*, AND TURNING, SAW MY GUARDIAN.

MISS HAVISHAM MADE A STRONG ATTEMPT TO *COMPOSE* HERSELF, AND STAMMERED THAT HE WAS AS PUNCTUAL AS EVER.

MISS HAVISHAM SENT US DOWN TO OUR *DINNER.* AS MR. JAGGERS AND I GROPED OUR WAY DOWN-STAIRS, HE TOLD ME MISS HAVISHAM *NEVER* ALLOWED HERSELF TO BE *SEEN* EATING OR DRINKING, BUT WANDERED ABOUT AT *NIGHT* AND THEN LAID HANDS ON SUCH FOOD AS SHE TOOK.

PRAY, SIR, MAY I ASK YOU A QUESTION?

ESTELLA'S *NAME*. IS IT *HAVISHAM* OR...

IT *IS* HAVISHAM.

AFTER DINNER, WE WENT UP TO MISS HAVISHAM'S ROOM, AND WE FOUR PLAYED AT *WHIST.*

WE PLAYED UNTIL NINE O'CLOCK, AND THEN IT WAS ARRANGED THAT WHEN *ESTELLA* CAME TO *LONDON* I SHOULD MEET HER *COACH.*

MY GUARDIAN LAY AT THE BOAR IN THE *NEXT* ROOM TO MINE. FAR INTO THE NIGHT, MISS HAVISHAM'S WORDS; *"LOVE HER, LOVE HER, LOVE HER!"* SOUNDED IN MY EARS. A BURST OF *GRATITUDE* CAME UPON ME, THAT SHE SHOULD BE *DESTINED* FOR *ME*, ONCE THE BLACKSMITH'S BOY.

THEN I TOOK *LEAVE* OF HER.

I NO LONGER THOUGHT THERE WAS ANYTHING *LOW* IN MY KEEPING AWAY FROM *JOE*, BECAUSE I KNEW ESTELLA WAS *CONTEMPTUOUS* OF HIM.

AFTER **CONSIDERING** THE MATTER WHILE DRESSING AT THE **BLUE BOAR** IN THE MORNING, I RESOLVED TO TELL MY GUARDIAN THAT I DOUBTED **ORLICK'S** BEING THE **RIGHT SORT** OF MAN TO FILL A POST OF **TRUST** AT MISS HAVISHAM'S.

VOLUME II
CHAPTER XI

WHY OF **COURSE** HE'S NOT THE RIGHT SORT OF MAN, PIP, BECAUSE THE MAN WHO FILLS THE POST OF TRUST **NEVER** IS THE RIGHT SORT OF MAN.

VERY GOOD, PIP. I'LL GO ROUND PRESENTLY, AND PAY OUR FRIEND **OFF**.

I WAS RATHER **ALARMED** BY THIS SUMMARY ACTION.

JAGGERS AND I TOOK THE MID-DAY COACH BACK TO LONDON. AS **SOON** AS I ARRIVED, I WENT ON TO BARNARD'S INN.

MY DEAR HERBERT, I HAVE SOMETHING VERY **PARTICULAR** TO TELL YOU.

HERBERT, I **LOVE** – I **ADORE** – ESTELLA.

WELL? OF **COURSE** I KNOW **THAT**.

HOW DO YOU KNOW IT? I NEVER **TOLD** YOU.

TOLD ME! WHY, WHEN YOU TOLD ME YOUR OWN STORY, YOU TOLD ME **PLAINLY** THAT YOU BEGAN ADORING HER THE FIRST TIME YOU **SAW** HER.

I SAW HER **YESTERDAY**. AND IF I ADORED HER BEFORE, I NOW **DOUBLY** ADORE HER.

LUCKY FOR **YOU** THEN, IF YOU ARE PICKED OUT AND **ALLOTTED** TO HER.

AND NOW, HANDEL, I WANT TO **REPAY** CONFIDENCE WITH **CONFIDENCE**. I WANT TO SAY A WORD OR TWO CONCERNING MY FATHER'S SON.

I AM **ENGAGED**.

BUT IT'S A **SECRET**. NAME OF **CLARA**.

PERHAPS I OUGHT TO MENTION THAT SHE IS RATHER **BELOW** MY MOTHER'S **NONSENSICAL** FAMILY NOTIONS. I THINK HER FATHER WAS A SPECIES OF PURSER. HE'S AN INVALID NOW.

I HAVE NEVER **SEEN** HIM, FOR HE HAS ALWAYS KEPT TO HIS ROOM OVERHEAD. BUT I HAVE **HEARD** HIM CONSTANTLY. HE MAKES TREMENDOUS **ROWS** --

-- ROARS, AND PEGS AT THE FLOOR WITH SOME **FRIGHTFUL** INSTRUMENT! *HA, HA, HA!*

THE **MOMENT** I BEGIN TO REALISE CAPITAL, IT IS MY INTENTION TO **MARRY** HER!

WE WARMLY SHOOK HANDS UPON OUR MUTUAL **CONFIDENCE**...

...AND WENT TO THE **THEATRE** TO SEE MR. WOPSLE IN DENMARK.

VOLUME II
CHAPTER XII

HAMLET
PRINCE OF DENMARK

HAYMARKET THEATRE

LEAVING THE THEATRE, IT OCCURRED TO ME – WAS I TO PLAY **HAMLET** TO MISS HAVISHAM'S **GHOST**?

VOLUME II
CHAPTER XIII

I am to come to London the day after tomorrow by the midday coach. I believe it was settled you should meet me?

Miss Havisham has that impression, and I write in obedience to it. She sends you her regard.

Yours, Estella.

I BEGAN HAUNTING THE COACH-OFFICE IN CHEAPSIDE **BEFORE** THE COACH HAD **LEFT** THE BLUE BOAR IN OUR **TOWN**. I HAD PERFORMED THE FIRST HALF-HOUR OF A WATCH OF FOUR OR FIVE HOURS, WHEN **WEMMICK** RAN AGAINST ME.

HALLOA, MR. PIP. I SHOULD HARDLY HAVE THOUGHT THIS WAS **YOUR** BEAT. I AM GOING TO **NEWGATE**.

WOULD YOU LIKE TO **SEE** THE PLACE? HAVE YOU **TIME** TO SPARE?

I HAD SO **MUCH** TIME TO SPARE THAT THE PROPOSAL CAME AS A **RELIEF**. WEMMICK WALKED AMONG THE PRISONERS AND EXCHANGED WORDS WITH MANY. AS MR. JAGGERS'S SUBORDINATE, HE WAS HIGHLY **POPULAR**.

HOW ARE YOU, COLONEL?

ALL RIGHT, MR. WEMMICK.

EVERYTHING WAS DONE THAT **COULD** BE DONE, BUT THE EVIDENCE WAS TOO **STRONG** FOR US.

YES, IT WAS TOO STRONG, SIR, BUT I DON'T **CARE**.

I THINK I SHALL BE **OUT** OF THIS ON MONDAY, AND AM **GLAD** TO HAVE THE CHANCE OF BIDDING YOU **GOODBYE**.

*The recorder's report is made to-day, and he is **sure** to be **executed** on Monday.*

I RETURNED TO THE COACH-OFFICE WITH SOME THREE HOURS ON HAND. I CONSUMED THE TIME THINKING OF *ESTELLA* COMING TOWARDS ME, AND THOUGHT WITH ABSOLUTE *ABHORRENCE* OF THE *CONTRAST* BETWEEN THE JAIL AND HER.

I WAS STILL SHAKING THE *PRISON DUST* OFF MY CLOTHES, AND EXHALING ITS AIR FROM MY LUNGS, WHEN I SAW HER *FACE* AT THE COACH WINDOW.

I AM GOING TO *RICHMOND.* I AM TO HAVE A *CARRIAGE,* AND *YOU* ARE TO TAKE ME. YOU ARE TO PAY MY *CHARGES* OUT OF MY PURSE.

VOLUME II
CHAPTER XIV

OH, YOU *MUST* TAKE IT! WE HAVE NO CHOICE, YOU AND I, BUT TO *OBEY* OUR INSTRUCTIONS.

WILL YOU *REST* HERE A LITTLE?

YES, I AM TO REST A LITTLE, AND DRINK SOME TEA, AND *YOU* ARE TO *TAKE CARE* OF ME THE WHILE.

HER TONE, AS IF OUR ASSOCIATION WERE *FORCED* UPON US, AND WE MERE *PUPPETS,* GAVE ME PAIN.

WHERE ARE YOU *GOING* TO, AT RICHMOND?

I AM GOING TO LIVE, AT A *GREAT* EXPENSE, WITH A LADY THERE, WHO HAS THE POWER OF TAKING ME ABOUT, AND *INTRODUCING* ME TO PEOPLE.

AND HOW DO YOU *THRIVE* WITH MR. POCKET?

I LIVE QUITE PLEASANTLY THERE – AT LEAST, AS PLEASANTLY AS I *COULD* ANYWHERE, AWAY FROM *YOU.*

AS I HAD GROWN **ACCUSTOMED** TO MY EXPECTATIONS, I HAD BEGUN TO NOTICE THEIR EFFECT UPON MYSELF AND THOSE **AROUND** ME.

THEIR INFLUENCE ON MY OWN CHARACTER WAS **NOT** GOOD.

I FURTHER PERCEIVED THAT MY EXPECTATIONS WERE NOT BENEFICIAL TO **HERBERT**.
MY LAVISH HABITS LED HIS EASY NATURE INTO **EXPENSES** THAT HE COULD NOT **AFFORD**.

WE GRADUALLY FELL INTO KEEPING LATE HOURS. AS WE GOT MORE AND MORE INTO **DEBT**, BREAKFASTS BECAME GLOOMIER AND GLOOMIER, BEING ON OCCASION THREATENED BY LETTER WITH **LEGAL** PROCEEDINGS.

MY DEAR HERBERT, WE ARE GETTING ON **BADLY**. LET US LOOK INTO OUR AFFAIRS.

WE ALWAYS DERIVED PROFOUND **SATISFACTION** FROM MAKING AN APPOINTMENT FOR THIS PURPOSE. I FELT I ESTABLISHED THE REPUTATION OF A FIRST-RATE MAN OF **BUSINESS** ON THESE OCCASIONS – PROMPT, DECISIVE AND COOL-HEADED.

slide

THERE WAS A **CALM**, A VIRTUOUS HUSH, AFTER THESE EXAMINATIONS.

IT'S FOR **YOU**, HANDEL. I HOPE THERE IS NOTHING THE MATTER.

THE LETTER WAS SIGNED TRABB & Cº, AND BEGGED TO INFORM ME THAT MRS. J. GARGERY HAD **DEPARTED** THIS **LIFE** ON MONDAY LAST...

...AND THAT MY ATTENDANCE WAS REQUESTED AT THE **INTERMENT** ON MONDAY NEXT AT THREE O'CLOCK.

THE FIGURE OF MY SISTER IN HER CHAIR BY THE FIRE **HAUNTED** ME NIGHT AND DAY.

I WROTE TO JOE TO OFFER CONSOLATION AND TO **ASSURE** HIM THAT I WOULD COME TO THE FUNERAL.

VOLUME II
CHAPTER XVI

DEAR JOE, HOW **ARE** YOU?

PIP, OLD CHAP, YOU KNOWED HER WHEN SHE WERE A **FINE FIGURE** OF A WOMAN.

Here they come!

Here they are!

WE WENT INTO THE CHURCHYARD, CLOSE TO THE GRAVES OF MY UNKNOWN **PARENTS**. THERE, MY SISTER WAS LAID **QUIETLY** IN THE **EARTH**.

AFTERWARDS, BIDDY, JOE, AND I HAD A COLD DINNER TOGETHER IN THE **BEST** PARLOUR. JOE WAS SO EXCEEDINGLY **PARTICULAR** WHAT HE DID WITH HIS KNIFE AND FORK, THAT THERE WAS GREAT **RESTRAINT** UPON US.

BUT HE WAS VERY MUCH **PLEASED** BY MY ASKING IF I MIGHT SLEEP IN MY **OWN** LITTLE ROOM, AND I FELT THAT I HAD DONE RATHER A **GREAT** THING IN MAKING THE REQUEST.

AS EVENING CLOSED IN, I TOOK **BIDDY** FOR A LITTLE **TALK**.

I SUPPOSE IT WILL BE **DIFFICULT** FOR YOU TO REMAIN HERE NOW, BIDDY DEAR?

OH! I CAN'T DO SO, MR. PIP.

HOW ARE YOU GOING TO **LIVE?** IF YOU WANT ANY MO--

HOW AM I GOING TO LIVE? I'LL **TELL** YOU, MR. PIP. I AM GOING TO TRY TO GET THE PLACE OF MISTRESS IN THE **NEW SCHOOL** NEARLY FINISHED HERE.

I HAVE NOT HEARD THE **PARTICULARS** OF MY SISTER'S DEATH, BIDDY.

THEY ARE VERY SLIGHT, **POOR** THING. SHE HAD BEEN IN ONE OF HER **BAD STATES** FOR FOUR DAYS, WHEN SHE SAID QUITE PLAINLY; "**JOE.**"

I **RAN** AND FETCHED MR. GARGERY, AND SHE LAID HER HEAD ON HIS SHOULDER. SHE PRESENTLY SAID "**JOE**" AGAIN, AND ONCE "**PARDON,**" AND ONCE "**PIP.**" AN HOUR LATER, SHE WAS **GONE.**

DO YOU KNOW WHAT IS BECOME OF ORLICK? HAVE YOU **SEEN** HIM?

WHY ARE YOU **LOOKING** AT THAT DARK TREE?

I SAW HIM **THERE** ON THE NIGHT SHE **DIED.** AND I HAVE SEEN HIM THERE, SINCE WE HAVE BEEN WALKING **HERE.** HE WAS NOT THERE A MINUTE, AND HE IS **GONE.**

I SHOULD THINK FROM THE **COLOUR** OF HIS CLOTHES THAT HE IS WORKING IN THE **QUARRIES.**

IT REVIVED MY UTMOST INDIGNATION TO FIND THAT SHE WAS STILL **PURSUED** BY THIS FELLOW.

I WILL TAKE **ANY** PAINS TO **DRIVE** HIM OUT OF THE **COUNTRY.**

BY DEGREES SHE LED ME INTO MORE **TEMPERATE** TALK.

YOU MUST KNOW THAT JOE **LOVES** YOU AND NEVER COMPLAINS ABOUT **ANYTHING**. HE DOES HIS DUTY WITH A **GENTLE** HEART.

BIDDY, WE MUST **OFTEN** SPEAK OF THESE THINGS, FOR I SHALL BE OFTEN DOWN HERE NOW. I AM NOT GOING TO LEAVE POOR JOE **ALONE**.

ARE YOU QUITE **SURE**, THEN, THAT YOU **WILL** COME TO SEE HIM **OFTEN?**

OH DEAR ME! THIS REALLY IS A VERY **BAD** SIDE OF HUMAN NATURE!

DON'T SAY ANY **MORE**, IF YOU PLEASE, BIDDY. THIS **SHOCKS** ME VERY MUCH!

I KEPT BIDDY AT A **DISTANCE** FOR THE REMAINDER OF THE EVENING.

AS OFTEN AS I WAS **RESTLESS** IN THE NIGHT, I REFLECTED WHAT AN INJURY, WHAT AN **INJUSTICE**, BIDDY HAD DONE ME. EARLY IN THE MORNING, I WAS TO GO.

GOOD-BY; DEAR JOE! – I SHALL BE DOWN **SOON**, AND **OFTEN**.

NEVER TOO **SOON**, SIR, AND **NEVER** TOO OFTEN, PIP.

BIDDY, I AM NOT ANGRY; BUT I AM **HURT**.

DON'T BE HURT – LET ONLY **ME** BE HURT, IF I HAVE BEEN **UNGENEROUS**.

ONCE MORE, THE MISTS WERE RISING AS I WALKED AWAY. IF THEY DISCLOSED TO ME THAT I SHOULD **NOT** COME BACK, AND THAT BIDDY WAS QUITE **RIGHT**, ALL I CAN SAY IS...

...THEY WERE QUITE **RIGHT** TOO.

85

HERBERT AND I WENT ON FROM BAD TO **WORSE**, IN THE WAY OF INCREASING OUR **DEBTS**.

TIME WENT ON, AND I CAME OF **AGE**. WE HAD LOOKED FORWARD TO MY ONE-AND-TWENTIETH **BIRTHDAY** WITH A CROWD OF **SPECULATIONS**, FOR WE BOTH CONSIDERED THAT MY GUARDIAN COULD HARDLY HELP SAYING SOMETHING **DEFINITE** ON THAT OCCASION.

I RECEIVED AN OFFICIAL NOTE FROM WEMMICK, INFORMING ME THAT MR. JAGGERS WOULD BE GLAD IF I WOULD CALL UPON HIM AT FIVE IN THE AFTERNOON OF THE AUSPICIOUS DAY. THIS CONVINCED US THAT SOMETHING **GREAT** WAS TO HAPPEN.

WELL, PIP – I MUST CALL YOU **MR. PIP** TODAY.

CONGRATULATIONS, MR. PIP.

NOW MY YOUNG **FRIEND**, I AM GOING TO HAVE A **WORD** WITH YOU.

WHAT DO YOU SUPPOSE YOU ARE LIVING AT THE **RATE** OF?

I AM UNABLE TO **ANSWER** THAT QUESTION.

I **THOUGHT** SO!

NOW, HAVE YOU **ANYTHING** TO ASK **ME**?

OF COURSE IT WOULD BE A GREAT RELIEF TO ME TO ASK YOU SEVERAL QUESTIONS, SIR, BUT I REMEMBER YOUR **PROHIBITION**.

IS MY **BENEFACTOR** TO BE MADE **KNOWN** TO ME TODAY?

NO. ASK ANOTHER.

HAVE -- I -- ANYTHING TO **RECEIVE**, SIR?

I THOUGHT WE SHOULD COME TO IT! YOU HAVE BEEN DRAWING PRETTY **FREELY** HERE; YOUR NAME OCCURS PRETTY **OFTEN** IN WEMMICK'S CASH-BOOK; BUT YOU ARE IN **DEBT**, OF COURSE?

I AM **AFRAID** I MUST SAY YES, SIR.

THAT IS A BANK-NOTE FOR **FIVE HUNDRED** POUNDS.

NOW, THAT HANDSOME SUM OF MONEY, PIP, IS YOUR **OWN** – A PRESENT TO YOU ON THIS DAY, IN EARNEST OF YOUR **EXPECTATIONS**.

AND AT THE **RATE** OF THAT SUM OF MONEY PER ANNUM, AND NO **HIGHER**, YOU ARE TO LIVE UNTIL THE DONOR OF THE **WHOLE** APPEARS.

THAT IS TO SAY, YOU WILL NOW TAKE YOUR MONEY AFFAIRS **ENTIRELY** INTO YOUR OWN HANDS.

MR JAGGERS, I HAVE **ANOTHER** QUESTION.

IS IT LIKELY THAT MY **PATRON** WILL SOON -- -- WILL SOON **COME** TO LONDON, OR **SUMMON** ME ANYWHERE **ELSE**?

COME! THAT'S A QUESTION I MUST **NOT** BE **ASKED** – A QUESTION THAT MIGHT **COMPROMISE** ME. THAT'S ALL I HAVE TO SAY.

FROM THIS LAST SPEECH I DERIVED THE NOTION THAT MISS HAVISHAM HAD **NOT** TAKEN HIM INTO HER **CONFIDENCE** AS TO HER DESIGNING **ME** FOR **ESTELLA**, AND THAT HE **RESENTED** THIS AND WOULD HAVE NOTHING TO DO WITH IT.

IF THAT IS **ALL** YOU HAVE TO SAY, SIR, THERE CAN BE **NOTHING** LEFT FOR **ME** TO SAY.

I WENT INTO THE OUTER OFFICE TO TALK TO WEMMICK.

MR. WEMMICK, I WANT TO ASK YOUR **OPINION**. I AM VERY DESIROUS TO SERVE A FRIEND.

THIS FRIEND IS TRYING TO GET **ON** IN COMMERCIAL LIFE, BUT HAS NO **MONEY**, AND FINDS IT DIFFICULT TO MAKE A **BEGINNING**.

NOW, I WANT SOMEHOW TO HELP HIM TO A **BEGINNING**, WITH SOME **MONEY** DOWN.

MR. PIP, THERE ARE **MANY** BRIDGES IN LONDON. **CHOOSE** YOUR BRIDGE, AND PITCH YOUR MONEY INTO THE **THAMES** OVER THE CENTRE ARCH, AND YOU KNOW THE END OF IT.

SERVE A FRIEND WITH IT, AND YOU MAY KNOW THE END OF IT TOO – BUT IT'S A LESS **PLEASANT** AND **PROFITABLE** END.

THEN IT IS YOUR **OPINION** THAT A MAN SHOULD **NEVER** --

INVEST **PORTABLE PROPERTY** IN A **FRIEND**? CERTAINLY HE SHOULD **NOT**. **UNLESS** HE WANTS TO GET **RID** OF THE FRIEND.

87

VOLUME II
CHAPTER XVIII

I DEVOTED THE NEXT SUNDAY AFTERNOON TO A *PILGRIMAGE* TO THE CASTLE.

I WAS ADMITTED BY THE *AGED*, WHO TOLD ME HIS SON WOULD *SOON* BE HOME FROM HIS AFTERNOON WALK. WE WENT IN AND SAT DOWN BY THE FIRESIDE.

THE OLD GENTLEMAN CHATTED IN HIS CHIRPING WAY, AND I *NODDED* AT HIM VIGOROUSLY. AFTER A GREAT DEAL OF NODDING, I WAS STARTLED BY A SUDDEN *CLICK* BY THE CHIMNEY...

Click

MY SON'S COME HOME!

John

WE WENT OUT TO THE DRAWBRIDGE AND THE AGED LOWERED IT. WEMMICK CAME ACROSS, AND PRESENTED ME TO *MISS SKIFFINS*.

MISS SKIFFINS SEEMED TO BE A *GOOD* SORT OF FELLOW, AND SHOWED A *HIGH REGARD* FOR THE AGED.

SHE WAS A *FREQUENT* VISITOR AT THE CASTLE; FOR WEMMICK SHOWED ME THAT THE INGENIOUS CONTRIVANCE BY THE CHIMNEY HAD A *SECOND* FLAP WITH *"MISS SKIFFINS"* ON IT.

Miss Skiffins John

WEMMICK INVITED ME TO TAKE A WALK ROUND THE PROPERTY; AND I **SEIZED** THE OPPORTUNITY. I INFORMED HIM THAT I WAS **ANXIOUS** ON BEHALF OF HERBERT POCKET. I TOLD HIM HOW HERBERT AND I HAD FIRST MET, AND GLANCED AT HIS HOME, CHARACTER, AND LACK OF MEANS.

I FEAR THAT HE MIGHT HAVE DONE **BETTER** WITHOUT ME AND MY EXPECTATIONS.

I HAVE GREAT **AFFECTION** FOR HERBERT. HOW CAN I BEST TRY TO HELP HIM TO SOME PRESENT INCOME AND GRADUALLY BUY HIM ON TO SOME SMALL PARTNERSHIP WITHOUT HIS **KNOWLEDGE?**

WELL YOU KNOW, MR. PIP, I MUST TELL YOU ONE THING. THIS IS DEVILISH **GOOD** OF YOU.

I'LL PUT ON MY CONSIDERING-CAP, AND I THINK ALL YOU WANT TO DO MAY BE DONE BY DEGREES. SKIFFINS (THAT'S HER BROTHER) IS AN **ACCOUNTANT** AND **AGENT**. I'LL LOOK HIM UP AND GO TO **WORK** FOR YOU.

I THANK YOU TEN THOUSAND TIMES.

BEFORE A **WEEK** WAS OUT, I RECEIVED A NOTE FROM WEMMICK, DATED WALWORTH, STATING THAT HE HAD MADE SOME **ADVANCE** IN THE MATTER.

THE UPSHOT WAS, THAT WE FOUND A WORTHY YOUNG SHIPPING-BROKER, ONE **CLARRIKER**, NOT LONG ESTABLISHED IN BUSINESS, WHO WANTED **CAPITAL**, AND, IN DUE COURSE OF TIME, A **PARTNER**.

BETWEEN HIM AND ME, **SECRET ARTICLES** WERE SIGNED OF WHICH HERBERT WAS THE SUBJECT. I PAID HIM **HALF** OF MY FIVE HUNDRED POUNDS DOWN, AND ENGAGED FOR SUNDRY OTHER PAYMENTS.

MISS SKIFFINS'S BROTHER **CONDUCTED** THE NEGOTIATION. WEMMICK PERVADED IT, BUT **NEVER APPEARED** IN IT. THE WHOLE BUSINESS WAS SO **CLEVERLY** MANAGED, THAT HERBERT HAD NOT THE **LEAST SUSPICION** OF IT.

I NEVER SHALL **FORGET** THE RADIANT FACE WITH WHICH HERBERT CAME HOME AND TOLD ME OF HIS HAVING FALLEN IN WITH ONE CLARRIKER, AND HIS BELIEF THAT THE **OPENING** HAD COME AT **LAST**.

DAY BY DAY, HIS HOPES GREW **STRONGER** AND HIS FACE **BRIGHTER**.

I HAD THE **GREATEST** DIFFICULTY IN RESTRAINING MY TEARS OF TRIUMPH WHEN I SAW HIM SO **HAPPY**.

VOLUME II
CHAPTER XIX

IF THAT **STAID** OLD HOUSE IN RICHMOND SHOULD EVER COME TO BE **HAUNTED** WHEN I AM DEAD, IT WILL BE HAUNTED, SURELY, BY **MY** GHOST. O, THE MANY, MANY NIGHTS AND DAYS THROUGH WHICH MY UNQUIET SPIRIT **HAUNTED** THAT HOUSE WHEN ESTELLA LIVED THERE!

THE LADY WITH WHOM SHE LIVED, MRS. BRANDLEY BY NAME, WAS A **WIDOW,** WHO HAD BEEN A **FRIEND** OF MISS HAVISHAM'S BEFORE HER **SECLUSION.**

BOTH IN AND OUT OF MRS. BRANDLEY'S HOUSE, I SUFFERED **EVERY** KIND OF **TORTURE** THAT ESTELLA COULD **CAUSE** ME.

SHE HAD ADMIRERS WITHOUT **END,** AND MADE USE OF ME TO **TEASE** THEM. SHE USED OUR VERY FAMILIARITY TO PUT A CONSTANT SLIGHT ON MY **DEVOTION.**

I SAW HER **OFTEN** AT RICHMOND...

PIP, PIP, WILL YOU **NEVER** TAKE **WARNING?**

OF **WHAT?** WARNING NOT TO BE ATTRACTED BY **YOU,** DO YOU MEAN, ESTELLA?

IF YOU DON'T **KNOW** WHAT I MEAN, YOU ARE **BLIND.**

PIP, MISS HAVISHAM **WISHES** TO HAVE ME FOR A DAY AT SATIS HOUSE. **YOU** ARE TO TAKE ME **THERE,** AND BRING ME **BACK,** IF YOU WILL.

CAN YOU TAKE ME? THE DAY AFTER TOMORROW, IF YOU PLEASE.

WE WENT DOWN ON THE NEXT DAY BUT ONE.

MISS HAVISHAM HUNG UPON HER **BEAUTY,** HER WORDS AND GESTURES, AS THOUGH SHE WERE **DEVOURING** HER.

HOW DOES SHE **USE** YOU, PIP; HOW **DOES** SHE USE YOU?

SHE EXTORTED FROM ESTELLA THE NAMES OF ALL THE MEN WHOM SHE HAD FASCINATED, AND DWELT UPON THE ROLL WITH WITCH-LIKE **EAGERNESS.**

I SAW IN THIS THAT ESTELLA WAS SET TO WREAK MISS HAVISHAM'S **REVENGE** ON MEN, AND THAT SHE WAS **NOT** TO BE GIVEN TO ME UNTIL SHE HAD **GRATIFIED** IT FOR A TERM.

IT HAPPENED ON THAT OCCASION THAT *SHARP* WORDS AROSE BETWEEN ESTELLA AND MISS HAVISHAM. IT WAS THE *FIRST* TIME I HAD EVER SEEN THEM *OPPOSED.*

WHAT! ARE YOU *TIRED* OF ME?

ONLY A LITTLE TIRED OF *MYSELF.*

SPEAK THE *TRUTH,* YOU *INGRATE!* YOU ARE *TIRED* OF *ME.* YOU *STOCK* AND *STONE!* YOU *COLD,* COLD *HEART!*

WHAT? DO YOU REPROACH ME FOR BEING *COLD?* I AM WHAT YOU HAVE *MADE* ME. TAKE ALL THE *PRAISE,* TAKE ALL THE *BLAME;*

IN SHORT, TAKE *ME.*

SO *PROUD!* SO *HARD!* BUT ESTELLA, TO BE PROUD AND HARD TO *ME!*

WHO *TAUGHT* ME TO BE PROUD? WHO *TAUGHT* ME TO BE HARD? I CANNOT *THINK* WHY YOU SHOULD BE SO UNREASONABLE WHEN I COME TO SEE YOU.

I HAVE *NEVER* FORGOTTEN YOUR WRONGS AND THEIR *CAUSES.* I HAVE NEVER BEEN *UNFAITHFUL* TO YOUR *SCHOOLING.*

I MUST BE *TAKEN* AS I HAVE BEEN *MADE.*

THE *SUCCESS* IS NOT MINE, THE *FAILURE* IS NOT MINE --

-- BUT THE TWO *TOGETHER* MAKE *ME.*

I TOOK *ADVANTAGE* OF THE MOMENT TO *LEAVE* THE ROOM.

WHEN I *RETURNED,* EVERYTHING WAS BACK TO *NORMAL.* WE PLAYED CARDS, AS OF YORE, AND SO THE EVENING WORE AWAY AND I WENT TO BED.

NEXT DAY THERE WAS NO *REVIVAL* OF THEIR DIFFERENCES, NOR WAS IT *EVER* REVIVED ON ANY SIMILAR OCCASION.

91

HERBERT AND I WERE ELECTED INTO A *CLUB* CALLED THE FINCHES OF THE GROVE, AND THE *FIRST* FINCH I SAW WAS *BENTLEY DRUMMLE*.

THE PRESIDING FINCH CALLED UPON MR. DRUMMLE TO TOAST A LADY. WHAT WAS MY INDIGNANT *SURPRISE* WHEN HE CALLED UPON THE COMPANY TO PLEDGE HIM TO...

ESTELLA OF RICHMOND, GENTLEMEN, AND A *PEERLESS* BEAUTY!

I *KNOW* THAT LADY.

AND SO DO *I.*

I BECAME HIGHLY *INCENSED* BY THIS, BUT SOON LEARNED HOW THEY HAD DANCED TOGETHER *SEVERAL* TIMES.

I CANNOT EXPRESS WHAT *PAIN* IT GAVE ME TO THINK THAT ESTELLA SHOULD SHOW *ANY* FAVOUR TO THIS CONTEMPTIBLE BOOBY. I SOON FOUND OUT THAT DRUMMLE HAD BEGUN TO FOLLOW HER *CLOSELY*, AND THAT SHE *ALLOWED* HIM TO DO IT.

SOON HE WAS *ALWAYS* IN PURSUIT OF HER, AND HE AND I CROSSED ONE ANOTHER EVERY DAY.

AT AN ASSEMBLY BALL AT RICHMOND, THE BLUNDERING DRUMMLE SO HUNG ABOUT ESTELLA AND WITH SO MUCH *TOLERATION* ON HER PART, THAT I RESOLVED TO *SPEAK* TO HER WHILE SHE WAITED FOR MRS. BRANDLEY TO TAKE HER HOME.

ESTELLA, *DO* LOOK AT THAT FELLOW IN THE CORNER *YONDER*, LOOKING OVER AT US.

WHY *SHOULD* I LOOK AT HIM? WHAT IS HE TO *ME?*

ESTELLA, DO *HEAR* ME SPEAK.

IT MAKES ME *WRETCHED* THAT YOU SHOULD ENCOURAGE A MAN SO GENERALLY *DESPISED* AS DRUMMLE.

PIP, DON'T BE *FOOLISH* ABOUT ITS *EFFECT* ON YOU. IT MAY HAVE ITS EFFECT ON *OTHERS*, AND MAY BE *MEANT* TO HAVE. IT'S NOT *WORTH* DISCUSSING.

DO YOU *DECEIVE* AND *ENTRAP* HIM, ESTELLA?

YES, AND *MANY* OTHERS – *ALL* OF THEM BUT *YOU.*

HERE IS MRS. BRANDLEY. I'LL SAY NO *MORE.*

92

A GREAT EVENT, THE *TURNING POINT* OF MY LIFE, NOW APPEARS IN VIEW. I WAS THREE-AND-TWENTY YEARS OF AGE, AND NOT ANOTHER *WORD* HAD I HEARD CONCERNING MY *EXPECTATIONS*.

VOLUME II
CHAPTER XX

IT WAS WRETCHED WEATHER, STORMY AND WET. I LOOKED THROUGH THE BLACK WINDOWS TO SEE THE LAMPS IN THE COURT WERE ALL *BLOWN OUT*.

HERBERT'S BUSINESS WAS STILL PROGRESSING, AND HAD TAKEN HIM ON A JOURNEY TO *MARSEILLES*, SO I WAS *ALONE*. MR. POCKET AND I HAD LONG PARTED COMPANY AS TO OUR ORIGINAL RELATIONS, THOUGH WE CONTINUED ON THE *BEST* TERMS.

NOTWITHSTANDING MY *INABILITY* TO SETTLE TO *ANYTHING*, I READ REGULARLY SO MANY HOURS A DAY. AT ELEVEN O'CLOCK, I HEARD A *FOOTSTEP* ON THE *STAIR*.

≋ CLUMP ≋

REMEMBERING THAT THE STAIRCASE LIGHTS WERE BLOWN *OUT*, I TOOK UP MY READING-LAMP AND WENT OUT. WHOEVER WAS BELOW HAD *STOPPED* ON SEEING MY LAMP, FOR ALL WAS *QUIET*.

THERE IS SOMEONE *DOWN* THERE, IS THERE NOT? WHAT FLOOR DO YOU *WANT*?

THE *TOP*.

MR. PIP.

THAT IS *MY* NAME. THERE IS NOTHING THE *MATTER*?

NOTHING THE MATTER.

I SAW A *FACE* THAT WAS *STRANGE* TO ME, LOOKING UP WITH AN INCOMPREHENSIBLE AIR OF BEING *PLEASED* BY THE *SIGHT* OF ME.

PRAY WHAT IS YOUR *BUSINESS?* DO YOU WISH TO COME *IN?*

YES, I WISH TO COME IN. I WILL *EXPLAIN* MY BUSINESS, MASTER.

93

94

WHERE WILL YOU **PUT** ME? I MUST BE PUT SOMEWHERES, TO SLEEP LONG AND SOUND. FOR I'VE BEEN **SEA-TOSSED** AND **SEA-WASHED**, MONTHS AND **MONTHS**.

MY FRIEND AND COMPANION IS **ABSENT**; YOU MUST HAVE HIS ROOM.

HE WON'T COME BACK **TOMORROW**; WILL HE? BECAUSE, LOOK'EE HERE, DEAR BOY, **CAUTION** IS NECESSARY. I WAS SENT FOR **LIFE**. IT'S **DEATH** TO COME BACK! I SHOULD OF A CERTAINTY BE **HANGED** IF TOOK.

AFTER HIS RUM AND BISCUIT SUPPER HE BADE ME **GOOD NIGHT** IN HERBERT'S ROOM. I SAT DOWN BY THE FIRE, AFRAID TO GO TO BED. I THEN BEGAN **FULLY** TO KNOW HOW **WRECKED** I WAS.

MISS HAVISHAM'S **INTENTIONS** TOWARDS ME, ALL A MERE **DREAM**.

ESTELLA **NOT** DESIGNED FOR ME; I ONLY SUFFERED IN SATIS HOUSE AS A **STING** FOR GREEDY **RELATIONS**.

SHARPEST AND DEEPEST PAIN OF ALL, IT WAS FOR THIS **CONVICT** THAT I HAD **DESERTED** JOE.

I SLEPT, WITHOUT PARTING FROM THE PERCEPTION OF MY **WRETCHEDNESS**.

WHEN I AWOKE, THE FIRE WAS **DEAD**, THE CANDLES **OUT**, AND THE **WIND** AND **RAIN** INTENSIFIED THE THICK BLACK **DARKNESS**.

WHAT IS YOUR **REAL** NAME?

MAGWITCH, CHRISEN'D **ABEL**.

WHEN YOU CAME HERE LAST NIGHT, AND ASKED THE WATCHMAN THE WAY; HAD YOU ANYONE **WITH** YOU? WAS ANYONE **ELSE** THERE?

WITH **ME**? NO, DEAR BOY. I DIDN'T TAKE PARTICULAR NOTICE, NOT KNOWING THE **WAYS** OF THE PLACE. BUT I THINK THERE **WAS** A PERSON, TOO, COME IN ALONGER ME.

WERE YOU **KNOWN** IN LONDON, ONCE? WERE YOU -- **TRIED** -- IN LONDON?

WHICH **TIME** - THE **LAST** TIME? YES, I FIRST KNOWED MR. **JAGGERS** THAT WAY. JAGGERS WAS **FOR** ME.

AND THIS IS THE **GENTLEMAN** WHAT I **MADE**! IT DOES ME GOOD FUR TO LOOK AT YOU, DEAR BOY!

I MUSTN'T SEE MY GENTLEMAN A **FOOTING** IT IN THE **MIRE** OF THE STREETS; THERE MUSTN'T BE NO **MUD** ON HIS BOOTS. MY GENTLEMAN MUST HAVE **HORSES**, PIP!

HORSES TO RIDE, AND HORSES TO DRIVE, AND HORSES FOR HIS SERVANT TO RIDE AND DRIVE AS **WELL**!

THERE'S SOMETHING WORTH **SPENDING** IN THAT THERE BOOK, DEAR BOY. IT'S YOURN. DON'T YOU BE **AFEERD** ON IT.

THERE'S **MORE** WHERE THAT COME FROM.

I'VE COME TO THE **OLD COUNTRY** FUR TO SEE MY GENTLEMAN SPEND HIS MONEY.

AND BLAST YOU **ALL**, FROM THE **JUDGE** IN HIS WIG TO THE **COLONIST** A STIRRING UP THE DUST - I'LL SHOW A **BETTER** GENTLEMAN THAN THE WHOLE KIT ON YOU PUT TOGETHER!

STOP! I WANT TO SPEAK TO YOU!

I WANT TO KNOW WHAT IS TO BE **DONE**. I WANT TO KNOW HOW YOU ARE TO BE KEPT OUT OF **DANGER**, HOW **LONG** YOU ARE GOING TO **STAY**!

HOW **LONG**? I'M NOT A GOING **BACK**. I'VE COME FOR GOOD! I'M NOT AFEERD TO PERCH UPON A SCARECROW. IF THERE'S **DEATH** HID INSIDE OF IT, LET HIM COME OUT, AND I'LL **FACE** HIM.

*IT APPEARED TO ME THAT I COULD DO NO BETTER THAN **SECURE** HIM SOME QUIET LODGING HARD BY, WHERE HE MIGHT STAY WHEN HERBERT **RETURNED**.*

I WAS **FORTUNATE** TO SECURE THE SECOND FLOOR OF A NEARBY LODGING-HOUSE FOR MY **UNCLE**, MR. PROVIS. THIS BUSINESS TRANSACTED, I TURNED MY FACE, ON MY OWN ACCOUNT, TO **LITTLE BRITAIN**.

NOW, PIP, BE **CAREFUL**. DON'T COMMIT **YOURSELF**, AND DON'T COMMIT **ANY** ONE. DON'T TELL ME ANYTHING: I DON'T WANT TO **KNOW** – I AM NOT **CURIOUS**.

HE **KNOWS** THE MAN HAS **COME!**

MR. JAGGERS, I MERELY WANT TO **ASSURE** MYSELF THAT WHAT I HAVE BEEN TOLD IS **TRUE**. I HAVE NO HOPE OF ITS BEING **UNTRUE**, BUT AT LEAST I MAY **VERIFY** IT.

BUT DID YOU SAY "**TOLD**" OR "**INFORMED**"? TOLD WOULD SEEM TO IMPLY VERBAL COMMUNICATION. YOU CAN'T HAVE **VERBAL** COMMUNICATION WITH A MAN IN **NEW SOUTH WALES**, YOU KNOW.

I WILL SAY, **INFORMED**, MR. JAGGERS. I HAVE BEEN INFORMED BY A PERSON NAMED **ABEL MAGWITCH**; THAT HE IS THE **BENEFACTOR** SO LONG UNKNOWN TO ME.

THAT IS THE MAN. IN **NEW SOUTH WALES**.

AND **ONLY** HE?

AND ONLY **HE**.

I AM NOT SO UNREASONABLE, SIR, AS TO THINK YOU AT ALL RESPONSIBLE FOR MY **MISTAKES** AND **WRONG CONCLUSIONS**; BUT I ALWAYS SUPPOSED IT WAS MISS **HAVISHAM**.

AS YOU SAY, PIP, I AM NOT AT **ALL** RESPONSIBLE FOR **THAT**.

WHEN MAGWITCH FIRST WROTE TO ME – FROM NEW SOUTH WALES – HE APPEARED TO HINT IN HIS LETTER AT SOME DISTANT IDEA OF **SEEING** YOU IN **ENGLAND**.

I CAUTIONED HIM THAT I MUST HEAR NO **MORE** OF THAT; THAT HIS PRESENTING HIMSELF HERE WOULD RENDER HIM LIABLE TO THE **EXTREME** PENALTY OF THE **LAW**. I GAVE MAGWITCH THAT CAUTION. HE GUIDED HIMSELF BY IT, NO DOUBT.

WE **WISHED** EACH OTHER A "GOOD DAY" AND SHOOK HANDS.

I RECOILED FROM PROVIS WITH A **STRONGER** REPULSION, THE **FONDER** HE BECAME OF ME.

WHEN HE WAS NOT ASLEEP, OR PLAYING PATIENCE WITH A RAGGED PACK OF CARDS, HE WOULD ASK ME TO **READ** TO HIM – "FOREIGN LANGUAGE, DEAR BOY!"

EXPECTING **HERBERT** ALL THE TIME, I DARED NOT GO **OUT**, EXCEPT WHEN I TOOK HIM FOR AN AIRING AFTER **DARK**.

THIS LASTED FOR ABOUT **FIVE DAYS**.

101

IN VAIN SHOULD I ATTEMPT TO DESCRIBE THE **ASTONISHMENT** OF HERBERT, WHEN HE AND I AND PROVIS SAT DOWN BEFORE THE FIRE, AND I RECOUNTED THE **SECRET**.

I SAW MY **OWN** FEELINGS REFLECTED IN HERBERT'S FACE, AND NOT LEAST AMONG THEM, **REPUGNANCE**.

HERBERT AND I WERE ANXIOUS FOR THE TIME WHEN PROVIS WOULD GO TO HIS **LODGING**; BUT HE SAT **LATE**. IT WAS **MIDNIGHT** BEFORE I TOOK HIM ROUND TO ESSEX STREET.

WHEN HIS **DOOR** CLOSED, I EXPERIENCED THE FIRST **RELIEF** I HAD KNOWN SINCE THE NIGHT OF HIS **ARRIVAL**.

STILL, SOMETHING MUST BE **DONE**. HE IS INTENT UPON VARIOUS NEW **EXPENSES** – HORSES, CARRIAGES, LAVISH APPEARANCES OF ALL KINDS. HE MUST BE **STOPPED** SOMEHOW.

YOU MEAN THAT YOU **CAN'T** ACCEPT --

-- HOW **CAN** I? THINK OF HIM! **LOOK** AT HIM! YET I AM AFRAID THE DREADFUL TRUTH IS THAT HE IS STRONGLY ATTACHED TO ME. WAS THERE **EVER** SUCH A **FATE**!

AFTER ALL, NEVER TAKING ANOTHER **PENNY** FROM HIM, THINK WHAT I **OWE** HIM ALREADY! THEN AGAIN: I AM HEAVILY IN **DEBT**, WHO HAVE NOW **NO EXPECTATIONS**.

I HAVE BEEN BRED TO **NO** CALLING --

-- AND AM FIT FOR **NOTHING**!

THE MAIN THING TO BE DONE, IS TO GET HIM **OUT** OF **ENGLAND**. YOU WILL HAVE TO GO **WITH** HIM, AND THEN HE MAY BE **INDUCED** TO GO.

THAT DONE, **EXTRICATE** YOURSELF, IN HEAVEN'S NAME, AND WE'LL SEE IT OUT **TOGETHER**, DEAR OLD BOY.

VOLUME III
CHAPTER III

NEXT MORNING, HE CAME ROUND AT THE APPOINTED TIME AND SAT DOWN TO HIS MEAL.

IN JAIL AND OUT OF JAIL, IN JAIL AND OUT OF JAIL, IN JAIL AND OUT OF JAIL. THAT'S *MY* **LIFE** PRETTY MUCH.

I'VE BEEN DONE **EVERYTHING** TO, PRETTY WELL – EXCEPT **HANGED**. I'VE BEEN PUT OUT OF TOWN, AND STUCK IN THE **STOCKS**, AND **WHIPPED** AND **WORRIED** AND **DROVE**.

I FIRST BECOME AWARE OF MYSELF DOWN IN **ESSEX**, A THIEVING **TURNIPS** FOR MY LIVING. SUMMUN HAD RUN AWAY FROM ME – A TINKER – AND HE'D TOOK THE FIRE WITH HIM, AND LEFT ME WERY **COLD**.

TRAMPING, BEGGING, THIEVING, **WORKING** WHEN I COULD – A BIT OF A POACHER, A BIT OF A LABOURER, A BIT OF A HAWKER, A BIT OF MOST THINGS THAT DON'T PAY AND LEAD TO **TROUBLE**, I GOT TO BE A **MAN**.

AT EPSOM RACES, OVER TWENTY YEARS AGO, I GOT ACQUAINTED WI' A MAN WHOSE **SKULL** I'D **CRACK**. HIS NAME WAS **COMPEYSON**; AND THAT'S THE MAN WHAT YOU SEE ME A **POUNDING** IN THE DITCH.

I WENT TO COMPEYSON AND HE TOOK ME ON TO BE HIS MAN AND **PARDNER**. AND WHAT WAS COMPEYSON'S **BUSINESS**? IT WAS SWINDLING, HANDWRITING FORGING, STOLEN BANK-NOTE PASSING, AND SUCH-LIKE. ALL SORTS OF **TRAPS** AS COMPEYSON COULD SET WITH HIS **HEAD**.

THERE WAS **ANOTHER** IN WITH COMPEYSON, AS WAS CALLED **ARTHUR**.

HE WAS IN A DECLINE, AND WAS A **SHADOW** TO LOOK AT.

HIM AND COMPEYSON HAD BEEN IN A **BAD** THING WITH A **RICH LADY** SOME YEARS AFORE. THEY'D MADE A **POT** OF MONEY BY IT, BUT HAD RUN THROUGH IT. ARTHUR WAS A **DYING** WITH THE **HORRORS** ON HIM, AND COMPEYSON'S WIFE (WHICH COMPEYSON **KICKED** MOSTLY) WAS A HAVING **PITY** ON HIM.

NOT TO GO INTO THE THINGS THAT COMPEYSON **PLANNED**, AND I **DONE** – I'LL SIMPLY SAY THAT THE MAN GOT ME INTO SUCH **NETS** AS MADE ME HIS **SLAVE**. I WAS ALWAYS IN **DEBT** TO HIM, ALWAYS A GETTING INTO **DANGER**.

HE WAS **YOUNGER** THAN ME, BUT HE'D GOT **CRAFT**; AND HE OVERMATCHED ME FIVE HUNDRED TIMES. MY **MISSIS** AS I HAD THE **HARD TIME** WI' --

-- **STOP**! I AIN'T BROUGHT **HER** IN --

HE LOOKED ABOUT HIM IN A **CONFUSED** WAY, AS IF HE HAD LOST HIS **PLACE** IN THE BOOK OF HIS **REMEMBERENCE**.

WINNE ENGLA

105

I RESOLVED NEVER TO BREATHE A **WORD** OF ESTELLA TO **PROVIS**. BUT BEFORE I COULD GO ABROAD, I FELT THAT I MUST **SEE** BOTH ESTELLA AND MISS HAVISHAM.

NEXT DAY, I SET OFF FOR MISS HAVISHAM'S BY THE EARLY MORNING COACH. WHEN WE DROVE UP TO THE BLUE BOAR, WHOM SHOULD I SEE, BUT **BENTLEY DRUMMLE**!

TO RICHMOND I WENT, BUT ESTELLA'S MAID TOLD ME THAT SHE HAD GONE TO **SATIS HOUSE**. SHE HAD NEVER YET GONE **WITHOUT ME** BEFORE.

YOU HAVE JUST COME **DOWN?**

BEASTLY PLACE – **YOUR** PART OF THE COUNTRY, I THINK?

YES, I AM TOLD IT IS VERY LIKE **YOUR** SHROPSHIRE.

NOT IN THE **LEAST** LIKE IT. LARGE TRACT OF **MARSHES**, I BELIEVE?

I AM GOING OUT FOR A RIDE, AND MEAN TO **EXPLORE**. CURIOUS LITTLE PUBLIC-HOUSES – AND SMITHIES – AND THAT.

HE CALLED TO THE WAITER, THEN **GLANCED** AT ME, WITH AN INSOLENT **TRIUMPH** ON HIS GREAT-JOWLED FACE.

IS THAT HORSE OF MINE **READY?**

LOOK HERE, YOU SIR. THE **LADY** WON'T RIDE TO-DAY; THE WEATHER WON'T **DO**. AND I DON'T **DINE**, BECAUSE I'M GOING TO DINE AT THE **LADY'S**.

MR. DRUMMLE, I DID NOT **SEEK** THIS CONVERSATION, AND I DON'T THINK IT AN **AGREEABLE** ONE.

WITH YOUR LEAVE, I WILL SUGGEST THAT WE HOLD **NO** KIND OF COMMUNICATION IN **FUTURE**.

QUITE **MY** OPINION. BUT DON'T LOSE YOUR **TEMPER**. HAVEN'T YOU LOST **ENOUGH** WITHOUT THAT?

YOU QUITE **UNDERSTAND** THAT THE YOUNG LADY DON'T RIDE TO-DAY; AND THAT **I** DINE AT THE **YOUNG LADY'S**.

WE SAT IN **SILENCE** UNTIL I WATCHED HIM LEAVE.

HEAVILY OUT OF SORTS, I WENT TO THE MEMORABLE OLD HOUSE.

WHAT WIND BLOWS YOU **HERE**, PIP?

MISS HAVISHAM, I WENT TO **RICHMOND** YESTERDAY TO **SPEAK** TO ESTELLA;

AND FINDING THAT SOME WIND HAD BLOWN HER **HERE**, I **FOLLOWED**.

WHAT I HAD TO SAY TO **ESTELLA**, MISS HAVISHAM, I WILL SAY BEFORE **YOU**, PRESENTLY. IT WILL **NOT** DISPLEASE YOU.

I AM AS **UNHAPPY** AS YOU CAN EVER HAVE MEANT ME TO BE.

I HAVE FOUND OUT WHO MY PATRON IS. IT IS NOT A **FORTUNATE** DISCOVERY, AND IS NOT LIKELY EVER TO ENRICH ME IN REPUTATION, STATION, FORTUNE, **ANYTHING**.

THERE ARE REASONS WHY I MUST SAY **NO MORE** OF THAT. IT IS NOT **MY** SECRET, BUT **ANOTHER'S**.

WHEN YOU FIRST CAUSED ME TO BE **BROUGHT** HERE, MISS HAVISHAM, I SUPPOSE I DID REALLY COME HERE, AS ANY CHANCE BOY MIGHT HAVE COME, LIKE A **SERVANT**, TO GRATIFY A **WHIM**, AND BE **PAID** FOR IT? AND MR. **JAGGERS** --

MR. JAGGERS HAD **NOTHING** TO DO WITH IT. HIS BEING **MY** LAWYER, AND HIS BEING THE LAWYER OF YOUR **PATRON**, IS A **COINCIDENCE**.

BUT WHEN I FELL INTO THE **MISTAKE** I HAVE SO LONG REMAINED IN, YOU LET ME GO **ON**. IN **HUMOURING** MY MISTAKE, YOU **PUNISHED** YOUR SELF-SEEKING RELATIONS.

I **DID**. WHY, THEY WOULD HAVE IT SO!

AND **YOU** MADE YOUR **OWN** SNARES. I NEVER MADE THEM.

I HAVE BEEN THROWN AMONG ONE FAMILY OF YOUR **RELATIONS**. AND I SHOULD BE **FALSE** IF I DID NOT TELL YOU, THAT YOU DEEPLY **WRONG** MR. MATTHEW POCKET AND HIS SON HERBERT, IF YOU SUPPOSE THEM TO BE OTHERWISE THAN **UPRIGHT**, OPEN, AND **INCAPABLE** OF ANYTHING DESIGNING OR MEAN.

WHAT DO YOU **WANT** FOR THEM?

ONLY THAT YOU WOULD NOT CONFOUND THEM WITH THE **OTHERS**.

I AM NOT SO **CUNNING**, AS I COULD HIDE FROM YOU THAT I **DO** WANT SOMETHING. MISS HAVISHAM, IF YOU WOULD SPARE THE MONEY TO DO MY FRIEND HERBERT A LASTING **SERVICE** IN LIFE.

I BEGAN THE SERVICE **MYSELF** MORE THAN TWO YEARS AGO, WITHOUT HIS KNOWLEDGE. WHY I **FAIL** IN MY ABILITY TO FINISH IT, I **CANNOT** EXPLAIN.

WHAT **ELSE?**

ESTELLA, YOU **KNOW** I **LOVE** YOU.

I HAVE **NO** HOPE THAT I SHALL EVER CALL YOU **MINE**, ESTELLA. STILL, I **LOVE** YOU. I HAVE **LOVED** YOU EVER SINCE I FIRST **SAW** YOU IN THIS HOUSE. IT WOULD HAVE BEEN HORRIBLY **CRUEL** IN MISS HAVISHAM, TO PRACTISE ON THE SUSCEPTIBILITY OF A POOR BOY, IF SHE HAD **REFLECTED** ON THE **GRAVITY** OF WHAT SHE DID.

YOU KNOW THAT I HAVE LOVED YOU **LONG** AND **DEARLY**. I SHOULD HAVE SAID THIS **SOONER**, BUT FOR MY LONG **MISTAKE**. IT INDUCED ME TO HOPE THAT MISS HAVISHAM **MEANT** US FOR ONE ANOTHER. WHILE I THOUGHT YOU COULD NOT HELP YOURSELF, I REFRAINED FROM **SAYING** IT. BUT I **MUST** SAY IT **NOW**.

BUT I THINK THAT IN THE ENDURANCE OF HER **OWN** TRIAL, SHE FORGOT **MINE**, ESTELLA.

IT SEEMS THAT THERE ARE **SENTIMENTS**, FANCIES – I DON'T KNOW HOW TO CALL THEM – WHICH I AM NOT ABLE TO **COMPREHEND**. WHEN YOU SAY YOU LOVE ME, I KNOW WHAT YOU MEAN AS A FORM OF **WORDS**, BUT NOTHING **MORE**. YOU TOUCH **NOTHING** IN MY BREAST.

I HAVE TRIED TO **WARN** YOU OF THIS; NOW, HAVE I NOT?

I HOPED YOU COULD NOT **MEAN** IT. SO YOUNG, UNTRIED, AND BEAUTIFUL, ESTELLA! **SURELY** IT IS NOT IN NATURE!

IT IS IN **MY** NATURE – IN THE NATURE FORMED WITHIN **ME**. I MAKE A GREAT **DIFFERENCE** BETWEEN **YOU** AND **ALL OTHER** PEOPLE WHEN I SAY SO MUCH.

I CAN DO NO **MORE**.

IS IT NOT **TRUE** THAT BENTLEY DRUMMLE IS IN TOWN HERE, AND **PURSUING** YOU? AND THAT YOU **ENCOURAGE** HIM, AND RIDE OUT WITH HIM, AND THAT HE DINES WITH YOU THIS VERY **DAY?**

YOU **CANNOT** LOVE HIM! YOU WOULD NEVER **MARRY** HIM, ESTELLA?

WHY NOT TELL YOU THE **TRUTH?**

I **AM** GOING TO BE MARRIED TO HIM.

TURNING FROM THE GATE, I GOT A LATE HACKNEY CHARIOT TO THE HUMMUMS IN COVENT GARDEN, WHERE A BED COULD BE GOT AT **ANY** HOUR OF NIGHT. THE CHAMBERLAIN SHOWED ME INTO A BEDROOM.

I GOT INTO BED AND LAY THERE WEARY AND **WRETCHED**, MY MIND MUCH OCCUPIED WITH THE QUESTION OF **WHY** I COULD NOT GO HOME, AND ALSO WITH THOUGHTS OF **ESTELLA**.

AT LAST I **DOZED** IN SHEER EXHAUSTION.

I HAD LEFT DIRECTIONS THAT I WAS TO BE CALLED AT SEVEN, FOR IT WAS PLAIN THAT I MUST SEE WEMMICK **IMMEDIATELY**.

HALLOA, MR. PIP! YOU **DID** COME HOME, THEN. WOULD YOU MIND TOASTING THIS **SAUSAGE** FOR THE AGED P.?

I SHOULD BE **DELIGHTED** TO DO IT.

NOW, MR. PIP. YOU UNDERSTAND WE ARE IN OUR **PRIVATE** AND PERSONAL CAPACITIES.

I ACCIDENTALLY HEARD, YESTERDAY MORNING, BEING IN A **CERTAIN** PLACE WHERE I ONCE TOOK YOU – IT'S AS WELL NOT TO MENTION NAMES –

THAT A CERTAIN PERSON OF **COLONIAL** PURSUITS HAD MADE SOME LITTLE STIR IN PART OF THE WORLD WHERE MANY PEOPLE GO, NOT ALWAYS IN GRATIFICATION OF THEIR OWN INCLINATIONS – BY DISAPPEARING, AND BEING NO MORE **HEARD** OF THEREABOUTS.

FROM WHICH, CONJECTURES HAD BEEN RAISED, AND **THEORIES** FORMED.

I ALSO HEARD THAT YOU HAD BEEN **WATCHED** AT YOUR CHAMBERS. BY WHOM, I WON'T GO INTO, AS IT MIGHT **CLASH** WITH **OFFICIAL** RESPONSIBILITIES.

AFTER A LITTLE MEDITATION, I TOLD HIM THAT I WOULD LIKE TO ASK A **QUESTION**, SUBJECT TO HIS ANSWERING OR NOT ANSWERING, AS HE DEEMED RIGHT. HE NODDED.

YOU HAVE HEARD OF A MAN OF BAD CHARACTER, WHOSE TRUE NAME IS **COMPEYSON**? IS HE **LIVING**? IS HE IN **LONDON**?

TO THESE QUESTIONS WEMMICK **NODDED**, AND WENT ON WITH HIS BREAKFAST.

NOW, QUESTIONING BEING **OVER**, I COME TO WHAT I **DID**. I WENT TO GARDEN COURT TO FIND YOU. **NOT** FINDING YOU, I WENT TO **CLARRIKER'S** TO FIND MR. HERBERT.

HIM I FOUND. WITHOUT MENTIONING ANY NAMES, I GAVE HIM TO UNDERSTAND THAT IF HE WAS AWARE OF **ANYBODY** – TOM, JACK, OR RICHARD – BEING ABOUT THE CHAMBERS OR NEIGHBOURHOOD, HE HAD BETTER GET HIM OUT OF THE **WAY**.

BUT I GAVE MY OPINION THAT IT WAS NOT SAFE TO TRY TO GET ANYONE **TOO** FAR OUT OF THE WAY AT PRESENT.

MR. HERBERT STRUCK OUT A **PLAN**. HE MENTIONED TO ME THAT HE IS COURTING A YOUNG LADY WHO HAS A BEDRIDDEN PA. WHICH PA LIES A-BED IN A BOW-WINDOW WHERE HE CAN SEE THE **SHIPS** ON THE RIVER.

THE HOUSE IS KEPT, IT SEEMS, BY A RESPECTABLE WIDOW WHO HAS A FURNISHED UPPER FLOOR TO LET. MR. HERBERT PUT IT TO ME, WHAT DID I THINK OF THAT AS A **TEMPORARY** TENEMENT FOR TOM, JACK, OR RICHARD?

I THOUGHT VERY **WELL** OF IT.

AFTER A WHILE AND WHEN **PRUDENT**, IF YOU **SHOULD** WANT TO SLIP ANYONE ON BOARD A FOREIGN **PACKET-BOAT**, THERE HE IS – READY.

WELL, SIR! MR. HERBERT **THREW** HIMSELF INTO THE BUSINESS, AND BY NINE O'CLOCK LAST NIGHT HE HOUSED TOM, JACK, OR RICHARD QUITE **SUCCESSFULLY**. AND NOW, MR. PIP, I HAVE PROBABLY DONE THE MOST I **CAN** DO.

THANK YOU FOR **ALL** YOUR HELP.

YOU ARE VERY WELCOME. I MUST BE OFF.

IF YOU HAD NOTHING MORE **PRESSING** TO DO THAN TO KEEP HERE TILL DARK, THAT'S WHAT I SHOULD ADVISE. IT WOULD DO YOU **GOOD** TO HAVE A PERFECTLY QUIET DAY WITH THE AGED.

*I SOON FELL **ASLEEP** BEFORE WEMMICK'S FIRE, AND WHEN IT WAS QUITE **DARK**, I LEFT THE AGED.*

ALL IS **WELL**, HANDEL. HE IS QUITE **SATISFIED**, THOUGH EAGER TO **SEE** YOU. MY DEAR GIRL IS WITH HER FATHER.

IF YOU'LL **WAIT** TILL SHE COMES DOWN, I'LL MAKE YOU KNOWN TO HER, AND THEN WE'LL GO UP-STAIRS.

THAT'S HER **FATHER**. I AM AFRAID HE IS A SAD OLD RASCAL, BUT I HAVE **NEVER** SEEN HIM. MRS. WHIMPLE IS THE **BEST** OF HOUSEWIVES, AND I REALLY DON'T KNOW WHAT MY CLARA WOULD DO WITHOUT HER MOTHERLY HELP. FOR, CLARA HAS NO MOTHER OF HER **OWN**, HANDEL, AND NO RELATION IN THE WORLD BUT OLD **GRUFFANDGRIM**.

SURELY THAT'S NOT HIS **NAME**, HERBERT?

NO, NO, THAT'S **MY** NAME FOR HIM. HIS NAME IS MR. BARLEY.

AS WE WERE CONVERSING IN A **LOW** TONE WHILE OLD BARLEY'S GROWL **VIBRATED** OVERHEAD, THE DOOR OPENED, AND A VERY PRETTY DARK-EYED GIRL CAME IN. HERBERT, **BLUSHING**, PRESENTED HER AS **CLARA**.

THERE WAS SOMETHING SO **NATURAL** AND WINNING, SO CONFIDING, **LOVING** AND INNOCENT, AND SOMETHING SO **GENTLE** IN HER THAT I WOULD NOT HAVE **UNDONE** THE ENGAGEMENT BETWEEN HER AND HERBERT FOR ALL THE **MONEY** IN THE POCKET-BOOK I HAD **NEVER** OPENED.

HERBERT ACCOMPANIED ME UP-STAIRS TO SEE OUR **CHARGE**. I FOUND PROVIS **COMFORTABLY** SETTLED IN TWO CABIN ROOMS AT THE TOP OF THE HOUSE. HE EXPRESSED NO **ALARM**, AND IT STRUCK ME THAT HE WAS **SOFTENED**.

I TOLD HIM HOW WEMMICK HAD HEARD IN NEWGATE PRISON THAT MY CHAMBERS HAD BEEN **WATCHED**; AND HAD RECOMMENDED HIS KEEPING **CLOSE** FOR A TIME, AND WHAT HE HAD SAID ABOUT GETTING HIM **ABROAD**.

...AND WHEN THE **TIME** COMES, I SHOULD GO **WITH** YOU.

113

WE ARE **BOTH** GOOD WATERMEN, HANDEL. WE COULD TAKE HIM DOWN THE RIVER **OURSELVES** WHEN THE TIME COMES.

IT MIGHT BE A GOOD THING IF YOU BEGAN TO KEEP A **BOAT** AT THE TEMPLE STAIRS, AND WERE IN THE HABIT OF **ROWING** UP AND DOWN. YOU FALL INTO THAT HABIT, AND THEN WHO **NOTICES** OR **MINDS?**

I **LIKED** THIS SCHEME, AND PROVIS WAS QUITE ELATED BY IT.

WE FURTHER AGREED THAT PROVIS SHOULD **WATCH** FOR US UPON THE RIVER, AND PULL DOWN THE **BLIND** IN THAT PART OF HIS WINDOW WHICH LOOKED EAST, WHENEVER HE SAW US AND ALL WAS **RIGHT.**

OUR CONFERENCE BEING ENDED, I ROSE TO **GO.**

I DON'T LIKE TO **LEAVE** YOU HERE, THOUGH I CANNOT DOUBT YOUR BEING SAFER **HERE** THAN NEAR **ME.** GOOD-BY!

DEAR BOY; I DON'T KNOW **WHEN** WE MAY MEET **AGAIN,** BUT I DON'T **LIKE** GOOD-BY. SAY **GOOD NIGHT!**

GOOD-NIGHT! HERBERT WILL GO **REGULARLY** BETWEEN US, AND WHEN THE TIME **COMES** YOU MAY BE **CERTAIN** I SHALL BE **READY.**

NEXT DAY I SET MYSELF TO GET THE **BOAT.** IT WAS BROUGHT ROUND TO THE TEMPLE-STAIRS, AND LAY WHERE I COULD **REACH** HER WITHIN A **MINUTE** OR TWO.

I BEGAN TO GO OUT AS FOR TRAINING AND PRACTICE: SOMETIMES **ALONE,** SOMETIMES WITH **HERBERT.**

THE FIRST TIME I PASSED MILL POND BANK, HERBERT AND I WERE PULLING A PAIR OF OARS. BOTH IN GOING AND RETURNING, WE SAW THE **BLIND** TOWARDS THE EAST COME **DOWN.**

STILL, I COULD NOT GET RID OF THE NOTION OF BEING **WATCHED.**

SOME WEEKS PASSED WITHOUT **CHANGE**. WE WAITED FOR WEMMICK, AND HE MADE NO **SIGN**. MY WORLDLY AFFAIRS BEGAN TO WEAR A **GLOOMY** APPEARANCE, AND I WAS PRESSED FOR **MONEY** BY **SEVERAL** CREDITORS.

I BEGAN TO RELIEVE THE WANT OF READY MONEY BY CONVERTING SOME **JEWELLERY** INTO **CASH**.

PLEDGE TOKENS

5/-

I HAD DETERMINED THAT IT WOULD BE A HEARTLESS **FRAUD** TO TAKE **MORE** MONEY FROM MY PATRON.

AS TIME WORE ON, AN IMPRESSION SETTLED UPON ME THAT ESTELLA WAS **MARRIED**. **FEARFUL** OF HAVING IT **CONFIRMED**, I AVOIDED THE NEWSPAPERS AND BEGGED HERBERT **NEVER** TO SPEAK OF HER.

IT WAS AN **UNHAPPY** LIFE, WITH ONE DOMINANT **ANXIETY**.

CONDEMNED TO SUSPENSE, I ROWED ABOUT IN MY BOAT...

...AND **WAITED**, WAITED, AS I BEST **COULD**.

LATE IN THE MONTH OF FEBRUARY, IT WAS A RAW EVENING – AND I THOUGHT I WOULD GO TO THE **PLAY** AND SEE **MR. WOPSLE**.

IT IS THE **STRANGEST** THING! YOU'LL HARDLY **BELIEVE** WHAT I AM GOING TO TELL YOU. YOU REMEMBER IN **OLD** TIMES A CERTAIN CHRISTMAS DAY, WHEN YOU WERE QUITE A CHILD AND THERE WAS A **CHASE** AFTER TWO **CONVICTS**?

YES, I REMEMBER **ALL** THAT.

THEN MR. PIP, ONE OF THOSE TWO PRISONERS SAT **BEHIND** YOU **TONIGHT**. THE ONE WHO HAD BEEN **MAULED** – I'LL SWEAR I **SAW** HIM!

I CANNOT **EXAGGERATE** THE ENHANCED DISQUIET INTO WHICH THIS CONVERSATION THREW ME, OR THE SPECIAL AND PECULIAR **TERROR** I FELT AT COMPEYSON'S HAVING BEEN BEHIND ME, "LIKE A **GHOST**".

WEMMICK AND I TOOK OUR LEAVE *EARLY*, AND *LEFT TOGETHER*.

WEMMICK, DO YOU REMEMBER TELLING ME, BEFORE I FIRST WENT TO MR. JAGGERS'S PRIVATE HOUSE, TO NOTICE THAT *HOUSEKEEPER*?

A WILD BEAST *TAMED*, YOU CALLED HER. *HOW DID* MR. JAGGERS TAME HER?

THAT'S HIS *SECRET*. SHE HAS BEEN WITH HIM *MANY* A LONG YEAR.

I WISH YOU *WOULD* TELL ME HER STORY – I FEEL A *PARTICULAR* INTEREST IN IT.

I DON'T KNOW *ALL* OF HER STORY, BUT WHAT I *DO* KNOW, I'LL *TELL* YOU.

A SCORE OR SO OF YEARS AGO, THAT WOMAN WAS *TRIED* AT THE OLD BAILEY FOR *MURDER*, AND WAS *ACQUITTED*.

SHE WAS A VERY HANDSOME YOUNG WOMAN. MR. JAGGERS WAS FOR HER, AND WORKED THE CASE IN A WAY QUITE *ASTONISHING*.

SHE LED A TRAMPING LIFE AND HAD MARRIED *YOUNG* "OVER THE BROOMSTICK".

IT WAS A CASE OF *JEALOUSY*. THE MURDERED PERSON WAS A WOMAN A GOOD TEN YEARS *OLDER*, AND MUCH LARGER AND *STRONGER*.

SHE WAS FOUND *DEAD* IN A BARN – THERE HAD BEEN A *VIOLENT* STRUGGLE. SHE WAS BRUISED AND SCRATCHED, AND HAD BEEN *CHOKED*.

THERE WAS *NO* REASONABLE EVIDENCE TO IMPLICATE *ANY* PERSON BUT *THIS* WOMAN.

THE PROSECUTION ATTEMPTED TO SET UP, IN PROOF OF HER JEALOUSY, THAT SHE WAS UNDER STRONG SUSPICION OF HAVING *DESTROYED* HER THREE-YEAR-OLD *CHILD* BY HER HUSBAND TO *REVENGE* HERSELF UPON HIM.

WELL, SIR! IT HAPPENED THAT THIS WOMAN WAS SO VERY *ARTFULLY* DRESSED FROM THE TIME OF HER APPREHENSION, THAT SHE LOOKED *SLIGHTER* THAN SHE REALLY *WAS*.

AND, ON THE *IMPROBABILITIES* OF HER BEING ABLE TO DO IT, MR. JAGGERS RESTED HIS CASE.

TO SUM UP, SIR, MR. JAGGERS WAS ALTOGETHER TOO MANY FOR THE *JURY*, AND THEY GAVE IN. IN FACT, THE CASE COULD ALMOST BE SAID TO HAVE *MADE* HIM.

SHE WENT INTO HIS SERVICE IMMEDIATELY AFTER HER ACQUITTAL, *TAMED* AS SHE IS NOW.

DO YOU REMEMBER THE *SEX* OF THE *CHILD*?

SAID TO HAVE BEEN A *GIRL*.

WE EXCHANGED A CORDIAL GOODNIGHT, AND I WENT HOME WITH *NEW* MATTER FOR MY THOUGHTS, THOUGH WITH NO *RELIEF* FROM THE OLD.

THE BEST LIGHT OF THE DAY WAS *GONE* WHEN I REACHED SATIS HOUSE. AN ELDERLY WOMAN, A *SERVANT*, OPENED THE GATE. I FOUND MISS HAVISHAM IN THE ROOM WITH THE GREAT TABLE, SITTING BY AN ASHY FIRE, *LOST* IN *CONTEMPLATION*.

THERE WAS AN AIR OF UTTER *LONELINESS* UPON HER, THAT MOVED ME TO *PITY*.

IT IS I, *PIP*. MR. JAGGERS GAVE ME YOUR NOTE *YESTERDAY*, AND I HAVE LOST *NO* TIME.

THANK YOU. I WANT TO *PURSUE* THAT SUBJECT YOU MENTIONED TO ME WHEN YOU WERE LAST HERE, AND TO SHOW YOU THAT I AM NOT *ALL* STONE.

YOU SAID, SPEAKING FOR YOUR *FRIEND*, THAT YOU COULD TELL ME HOW TO DO SOMETHING *USEFUL* AND *GOOD*.

I EXPLAINED TO HER THE SECRET HISTORY OF THE *PARTNERSHIP*. I TOLD HER HOW I HAD HOPED TO COMPLETE THE TRANSACTION OUT OF MY MEANS, BUT HOW I WAS *DISAPPOINTED*.

SO. AND HOW *MUCH* MONEY IS WANTING TO *COMPLETE* THE PURCHASE?

NINE HUNDRED POUNDS.

IF I GIVE YOU MONEY FOR THIS PURPOSE, YOU WILL KEEP *MY* SECRET AS YOU HAVE KEPT YOUR *OWN*?

QUITE AS FAITHFULLY.

YOU ARE STILL ON *FRIENDLY* TERMS WITH MR. JAGGERS?

QUITE. I *DINED* WITH HIM YESTERDAY.

THIS IS AN AUTHORITY TO HIM TO PAY YOU THE *MONEY* FOR YOUR FRIEND. BUT IS THERE *NOTHING* I CAN DO FOR YOU YOURSELF?

THANK YOU, MISS HAVISHAM. AND THANK YOU FOR THE *QUESTION*, BUT THERE IS NOTHING.

MY *NAME* IS ON THE FIRST LEAF. IF YOU CAN EVER WRITE UNDER MY NAME, "I FORGIVE HER", THOUGH EVER SO LONG AFTER MY BROKEN HEART IS *DUST* – PRAY DO IT!

O MISS HAVISHAM, I CAN DO IT *NOW*.

THERE HAVE BEEN SORE *MISTAKES*; AND MY LIFE HAS BEEN A *BLIND* AND *THANKLESS* ONE; BUT I WANT FORGIVENESS AND DIRECTION FAR TOO MUCH, TO BE *BITTER* WITH *YOU*.

TO SEE HER WITH HER WORN FACE KNEELING AT MY **FEET** GAVE ME A SHOCK THROUGH ALL MY FRAME. I ENTREATED HER TO **RISE**, BUT SHE **WEPT** DOWN UPON THE GROUND.

O! WHAT HAVE I **DONE!**

WHAT HAVE I DONE!

UNTIL YOU **SPOKE** THE OTHER DAY, AND I SAW IN YOU A LOOKING-GLASS THAT SHOWED ME WHAT I **ONCE** FELT **MYSELF**, I DID NOT **KNOW** WHAT I HAD DONE.

BUT, PIP – MY DEAR! BELIEVE **THIS:** WHEN SHE FIRST CAME TO ME, I MEANT TO **SAVE** HER FROM **MISERY** LIKE MY OWN.

AT FIRST, I MEANT NO **MORE.**

BUT AS SHE **GREW,** AND PROMISED TO BE **BEAUTIFUL,** I GRADUALLY DID WORSE. WITH MY PRAISES, MY JEWELS, AND MY TEACHINGS, I STOLE HER **HEART** AWAY --

-- AND PUT **ICE** IN ITS PLACE.

WELL, **WELL!** BUT IF YOU CAN EVER UNDO ANY **SCRAP** OF WHAT YOU HAVE DONE AMISS IN KEEPING HER **RIGHT** NATURE FROM HER, IT WILL BE BETTER TO DO **THAT** --

-- THAN TO BEMOAN THE **PAST** THROUGH A HUNDRED YEARS.

MISS HAVISHAM, DOES WHAT HAS PASSED **BETWEEN** US GIVE ME ANY **EXCUSE** FOR ASKING YOU A QUESTION RELATIVE TO ESTELLA, AS SHE WAS WHEN SHE **FIRST** CAME HERE?

GO ON.

WHOSE CHILD WAS **ESTELLA?**

I DON'T **KNOW.** I HAD BEEN SHUT UP IN THESE ROOMS A **LONG** TIME, WHEN I TOLD MR. JAGGERS THAT I WANTED A LITTLE GIRL TO REAR AND **SAVE** FROM **MY** FATE.

ONE NIGHT HE BROUGHT HER HERE **ASLEEP,** AND I CALLED HER ESTELLA.

SHE WAS THEN TWO OR THREE. SHE KNOWS ONLY THAT SHE WAS LEFT AN **ORPHAN,** AND I **ADOPTED** HER.

WE PARTED. **TWILIGHT** WAS CLOSING IN WHEN I WENT DOWNSTAIRS. I DECIDED TO WALK ROUND THE OLD PLACE BEFORE **LEAVING,** FOR I HAD A PRESENTIMENT THAT I SHOULD NEVER BE THERE **AGAIN.**

I WENT ALL ROUND THE RUINED GARDEN, THEN RAISED THE RUSTY LATCH AND PASSED INTO THE **BREWERY.**

BREWERY

I CLOSED WITH HER, *THREW* HER DOWN, AND GOT MY *GREAT-COAT* OVER HER.

I DRAGGED THE CLOTH FROM THE *TABLE*, AND WITH IT THE HEAP OF ROTTENNESS.

CLANK!

CHINK!

THEN WE WERE ON THE GROUND *STRUGGLING* LIKE DESPERATE ENEMIES.

121

SHE WAS *INSENSIBLE*, AND I WAS AFRAID TO HAVE HER MOVED OR TOUCHED. ASSISTANCE WAS SENT FOR, AND I *HELD* HER UNTIL IT *CAME*.

ON THE SURGEON'S COMING, I GOT UP, AND WAS ASTONISHED TO SEE THAT BOTH MY *HANDS* WERE *BURNT*; FOR I HAD NO *KNOWLEDGE* OF IT THROUGH FEELING.

THE SURGEON PRONOUNCED THAT SHE HAD RECEIVED *SERIOUS* HURTS, BUT THE MAIN DANGER LAY IN THE *NERVOUS SHOCK*.

AS I COULD DO NO *SERVICE* THERE, I DECIDED IN THE COURSE OF THE NIGHT, THAT I WOULD *RETURN* BY THE EARLY MORNING COACH.

AT ABOUT SIX O'CLOCK OF THE MORNING, THEREFORE, I LEANED OVER HER AND *TOUCHED* HER LIPS WITH *MINE*, JUST AS SHE SAID...

Take the pencil and write under my name, "I Forgive her."

BACK AT OUR CHAMBERS, HERBERT DEVOTED THE DAY TO ATTENDING ON ME. HE WAS THE KINDEST OF NURSES, TAKING OFF THE BANDAGES, STEEPING THEM IN COOLING LIQUID AND REPLACING THEM WITH PATIENT TENDERNESS.

IS ALL WELL DOWN THE RIVER?

YES – I SAT WITH PROVIS LAST NIGHT, HANDEL, TWO GOOD HOURS. HE WAS VERY COMMUNICATIVE; AND TOLD ME MORE OF HIS LIFE. YOU REMEMBER HIS BREAKING OFF HERE ABOUT SOME WOMAN THAT HE HAD HAD GREAT TROUBLE WITH?

WELL! IT SEEMS THAT THE WOMAN WAS A YOUNG WOMAN, JEALOUS AND REVENGEFUL – REVENGEFUL TO THE LAST DEGREE.

TO WHAT LAST DEGREE?

MURDER.

VOLUME III CHAPTER XI

SHE WAS TRIED FOR IT, AND MR. JAGGERS DEFENDED HER. THAT DEFENCE FIRST MADE HIS NAME KNOWN TO PROVIS. IT WAS ANOTHER, STRONGER, WOMAN WHO WAS THE VICTIM, AND THERE HAD BEEN A STRUGGLE – IN A BARN. THE VICTIM WAS FOUND THROTTLED. BUT THE WOMAN WAS ACQUITTED. THIS YOUNG WOMAN AND PROVIS HAD A CHILD, OF WHOM PROVIS WAS EXCEEDINGLY FOND.

ON THE NIGHT IN QUESTION, THE YOUNG WOMAN PRESENTED HERSELF BEFORE PROVIS FOR ONE MOMENT, SWORE THAT SHE WOULD DESTROY THE CHILD, AND HE SHOULD NEVER SEE IT AGAIN; THEN, SHE VANISHED.

DID THE WOMAN KEEP HER OATH?

HE SAYS THAT SHE DID.

FEARING THAT HE SHOULD BE CALLED UPON TO DEPOSE ABOUT THE CHILD, AND SO BE THE CAUSE OF HER DEATH, HE HID HIMSELF OUT OF THE WAY, AND WAS ONLY VAGUELY TALKED OF AS A MAN CALLED ABEL, OUT OF WHOM THE JEALOUSY AROSE.

AFTER THE ACQUITTAL SHE DISAPPEARED.

HERBERT, DID HE TELL YOU WHEN THIS HAPPENED?

PARTICULARLY? HIS EXPRESSION WAS, "A ROUND SCORE O' YEAR AGO." HE SAID THAT IT HAD HAPPENED SOME THREE OR FOUR YEARS BEFORE HE CAME UPON YOU IN THE CHURCHYARD, AND YOU BROUGHT INTO HIS MIND THE LITTLE GIRL SO TRAGICALLY LOST, WHO WOULD HAVE BEEN ABOUT YOUR AGE.

HERBERT, LOOK AT ME. I AM NOT IN ANY FEVER, AND KNOW I AM QUITE MYSELF. THE MAN WE HAVE IN HIDING DOWN THE RIVER --

-- IS ESTELLA'S FATHER.

WHAT **PURPOSE** I HAD IN VIEW IN **TRACING** ESTELLA'S PARENTAGE, I CANNOT SAY. BUT I WAS **SEIZED** WITH A FEVERISH CONVICTION THAT I **OUGHT** TO HUNT THE MATTER DOWN, AND SEE MR. JAGGERS AND COME AT THE BARE **TRUTH**.

EARLY NEXT MORNING, I TOOK MY WAY TO LITTLE BRITAIN, AND FOUND MR. JAGGERS AND WEMMICK **TOGETHER**, GOING OVER THE OFFICE ACCOUNTS.

I PRODUCED MISS HAVISHAM'S **AUTHORITY** TO RECEIVE THE NINE HUNDRED POUNDS FOR HERBERT.

MR. JAGGERS'S EYES RETIRED **DEEPER** INTO HIS HEAD WHEN I HANDED HIM THE TABLETS, BUT HE GAVE THEM TO WEMMICK TO DRAW THE CHEQUE.

I AM SORRY THAT WE DO NOTHING FOR **YOU**, PIP.

MISS HAVISHAM WAS GOOD ENOUGH TO ASK WHETHER SHE COULD **DO** NOTHING FOR ME, AND I TOLD HER **NO**.

I **DID** ASK SOMETHING OF MISS HAVISHAM, HOWEVER. I ASKED HER TO GIVE ME SOME **INFORMATION** RELATIVE TO HER ADOPTED DAUGHTER --

-- AND SHE GAVE ME **ALL** SHE POSSESSED.

I KNOW MORE OF THE **HISTORY** OF MISS HAVISHAM'S ADOPTED **CHILD** THAN MISS HAVISHAM **HERSELF** DOES, SIR. I KNOW HER **MOTHER**.

MOTHER?

I HAVE **SEEN** HER MOTHER WITHIN THESE **THREE** DAYS. AND YOU HAVE SEEN HER STILL MORE **RECENTLY**.

PERHAPS I KNOW **MORE** OF ESTELLA'S HISTORY THAN EVEN **YOU** DO. I KNOW HER **FATHER** TOO.

A CERTAIN STOP THAT MR. JAGGERS CAME TO IN HIS MANNER **ASSURED** ME THAT HE DID **NOT** KNOW WHO HER FATHER WAS. THIS I HAD SUSPECTED FROM PROVIS'S ACCOUNT, HAVING PIECED TOGETHER THAT HE WAS NOT MR. JAGGERS'S CLIENT UNTIL SOME FOUR YEARS **LATER**.

SO! YOU KNOW THE YOUNG LADY'S **FATHER**, PIP?

YES, AND HIS NAME IS **PROVIS** – FROM NEW SOUTH WALES.

EVEN MR. JAGGERS **STARTED** WHEN I SAID THOSE WORDS.

AND ON WHAT **EVIDENCE**, PIP, DOES PROVIS MAKE THIS CLAIM?

HE DOES **NOT** MAKE IT, AND HAS **NEVER** MADE IT, AND HAS NO **KNOWLEDGE** THAT HIS DAUGHTER IS IN EXISTENCE.

PIP, I'LL PUT A **CASE** TO YOU. MIND! I ADMIT **NOTHING**. PUT THE CASE THAT A WOMAN, UNDER SUCH CIRCUMSTANCES AS YOU HAVE MENTIONED, HELD HER CHILD CONCEALED, AND COMMUNICATED THE FACT TO HER **LEGAL ADVISER**.

PUT THE CASE THAT, AT THE **SAME** TIME, HE HELD A TRUST TO **FIND** A CHILD FOR AN ECCENTRIC RICH LADY TO **ADOPT**.

I **FOLLOW** YOU, SIR.

PUT THE CASE THAT HE **OFTEN** SAW CHILDREN SOLEMNLY TRIED AT A CRIMINAL BAR, AND HABITUALLY **KNEW** OF THEIR BEING IMPRISONED, WHIPPED, TRANSPORTED, NEGLECTED,

CAST OUT, QUALIFIED IN **ALL** WAYS FOR THE **HANGMAN**, AND GROWING UP TO BE **HANGED**.

PUT THE CASE, **PIP**, THAT HERE WAS ONE **PRETTY** LITTLE CHILD OUT OF THE HEAP WHO **COULD** BE **SAVED**; WHOM THE FATHER BELIEVED **DEAD**, AND THAT THE WOMAN WAS **CLEARED**.

I UNDERSTAND YOU **PERFECTLY**.

PUT THE **CASE**, PIP, THAT PASSION AND THE TERROR OF DEATH HAD A LITTLE **SHAKEN** THE WOMAN'S **INTELLECTS**, AND THAT WHEN SHE WAS SET AT LIBERTY, SHE WENT TO HIM TO BE **SHELTERED**.

PUT THE CASE THAT HE TOOK HER IN, AND KEPT DOWN THE WILD, **VIOLENT** NATURE BY ASSERTING HIS OLD **POWER** OVER HER.

PUT THE CASE THAT THE CHILD **GREW UP**, AND WAS **MARRIED**.

THAT THE MOTHER AND THE FATHER WERE STILL **LIVING**; AND, **UNKNOWN** TO ONE ANOTHER, DWELLING WITHIN SO MANY MILES OF ONE ANOTHER.

THAT THE SECRET WAS **STILL** A SECRET, EXCEPT THAT **YOU** HAD GOT WIND OF IT.

FOR **WHOSE** SAKE WOULD YOU **REVEAL** THE SECRET? FOR THE **FATHER'S**? FOR THE **MOTHER'S**? I THINK **NOT**. FOR THE **DAUGHTER'S**? I THINK IT WOULD HARDLY **SERVE** HER TO DRAG HER BACK TO **DISGRACE**.

ADD THE CASE THAT YOU HAD **LOVED** HER, PIP, AND I TELL YOU THAT YOU HAD BETTER **CHOP OFF** BOTH THOSE BANDAGED **HANDS** OF YOURS.

NOW, WEMMICK, WHAT ITEM **WAS** IT YOU WERE AT WHEN MR. PIP CAME IN?

SO MR. JAGGERS AND WEMMICK WENT TO WORK AGAIN WITH AN AIR OF **REFRESHMENT** UPON THEM AS IF THEY HAD JUST HAD **LUNCH**.

I WENT, WITH MY CHEQUE IN MY **POCKET**, TO MISS SKIFFINS'S BROTHER; AND WE WENT STRAIGHT TO **CLARRIKER**.

CLARRIKER INFORMED THAT HIS AFFAIRS WERE **STEADILY PROGRESSING**, AND THAT HE WOULD **NOW** BE ABLE TO ESTABLISH A BRANCH-HOUSE IN THE **EAST**. HERBERT IN HIS **NEW CAPACITY** WOULD GO OUT AND TAKE **CHARGE** OF IT.

I FELT AS IF MY LAST **ANCHOR** WERE LOOSENING ITS HOLD; BUT THERE WAS RECOMPENSE IN THE **JOY** WITH WHICH HERBERT WOULD COME HOME AND TELL ME OF THESE **CHANGES**.

WE HAD NOW GOT WELL INTO **MARCH**. MY LEFT ARM WAS TAKING A LONG TIME TO HEAL, THOUGH MY RIGHT ARM WAS TOLERABLY **RESTORED**.

ON A MONDAY MORNING, WHEN HERBERT AND I WERE AT BREAKFAST, I RECEIVED THE FOLLOWING **LETTER** FROM WEMMICK BY THE POST...

Walworth.
Burn this as soon as read. Early in the week, or say Wednesday, you might do what you know of, if you felt disposed to try it.
Now Burn.

WHEN I HAD SHOWN THIS TO HERBERT, WE CONSIDERED WHAT TO **DO**. FOR OF COURSE, MY BEING **DISABLED** COULD NOW BE NO LONGER KEPT OUT OF VIEW.

I HAVE **THOUGHT** IT OVER AGAIN AND AGAIN, AND I THINK WE SHOULD TAKE **STARTOP**. A GOOD FELLOW, A SKILLED HAND, FOND OF US AND **HONOURABLE**. IT IS NECESSARY TO TELL HIM VERY **LITTLE**.

AS FOREIGN STEAMERS WOULD **LEAVE** LONDON AT ABOUT HIGH-WATER, OUR PLAN WAS TO GET DOWN THE RIVER BY A **PREVIOUS** EBB-TIDE, AND **LIE BY** IN SOME QUIET SPOT UNTIL WE COULD PULL OFF TO ONE.

WE WENT OUT AFTER BREAKFAST TO **PURSUE** OUR INVESTIGATIONS. WE FOUND THAT A STEAMER FOR **HAMBURG** WAS LIKELY TO SUIT OUR PURPOSE BEST, BUT NOTED DOWN WHAT **OTHER** STEAMERS WOULD LEAVE LONDON WITH THE SAME TIDE.

THEN SEPARATED FOR A FEW HOURS: I, TO GET SUCH PASSPORTS AS WERE **NECESSARY**; HERBERT, TO SEE **STARTOP** AT HIS LODGINGS.

WHEN WE MET AGAIN, HERBERT SAID THAT STARTOP WAS **MORE** THAN READY TO JOIN. WE ARRANGED THAT HERBERT SHOULD PREPARE PROVIS TO COME DOWN TO THE STAIRS HARD BY THE HOUSE, ON WEDNESDAY, WHEN HE SAW US **APPROACH**.

HAVING MADE OUR ARRANGEMENTS, I WENT HOME. THERE, I FOUND A **LETTER** DIRECTED TO **ME** – A **DIRTY** LETTER, THOUGH NOT ILL-WRITTEN. IT HAD BEEN DELIVERED BY **HAND**.

IF YOU ARE NOT AFRAID TO COME TO THE MARSHES TONIGHT OR TOMORROW NIGHT AT NINE, COME TO THE SLUICE-HOUSE BY THE LIMEKILN. IF YOU WANT INFORMATION REGARDING YOUR UNCLE PROVIS, YOU HAD BETTER COME AND TELL NO ONE. YOU MUST COME ALONE.

BRING THIS WITH YOU.

WHAT TO DO **NOW**, I COULD NOT TELL. AND THE WORST WAS, THAT I MUST DECIDE **QUICKLY**, OR MISS THE AFTERNOON COACH. THE REFERENCE TO PROVIS TURNED THE SCALE, AND I RESOLVED TO **GO**.

I LEFT A NOTE FOR **HERBERT**, TELLING HIM THAT AS I WAS GOING **AWAY**, I HAD DECIDED TO HURRY DOWN TO ASCERTAIN HOW MISS **HAVISHAM** WAS **FARING**.

I CAUGHT THE COACH JUST AS IT CAME OUT OF THE YARD. IT WAS **DARK** BEFORE WE GOT DOWN. I WENT TO SATIS HOUSE AND **INQUIRED** FOR MISS HAVISHAM; SHE WAS STILL VERY **ILL**.

I SOUGHT IN MY POCKETS FOR THE **LETTER**, BUT COULD NOT FIND IT.

I KNEW **VERY WELL**, HOWEVER, THE APPOINTED **PLACE** AND THE **HOUR**. TOWARDS THE MARSHES I NOW WENT STRAIGHT, HAVING NO TIME TO **SPARE**.

AFTER A **BLANK**, I FOUND THAT I WAS LYING UNBOUND ON THE FLOOR, WITH MY HEAD ON SOMEONE'S **KNEE**, AND LOOKING AT A **FACE** — THE FACE OF TRABB'S BOY!

I **THINK** HE'S ALL RIGHT, BUT AIN'T HE JUST **PALE** THOUGH!

HERBERT! GREAT HEAVEN!

AND OUR OLD COMRADE, **STARTOP!**

MY DEAR HANDEL, WHAT **HURT** HAVE YOU GOT? CAN YOU **STAND?**

YES, YES, I CAN **WALK.** I HAVE **NO** HURT BUT THIS THROBBING **ARM.**

ENTREATING HERBERT TO TELL ME **HOW** HE HAD COME TO MY **RESCUE,** I LEARNT THAT I HAD IN MY HURRY **DROPPED** THE LETTER, **OPEN,** IN OUR CHAMBERS.

COMING HOME WITH STARTOP, HE HAD **FOUND** IT.

TRABB'S BOY HAD SEEN ME PASSING MISS HAVISHAM'S, AND BECAME THEIR **GUIDE** TO THE SLUICE-HOUSE.

WE RELINQUISHED ALL THOUGHTS OF **PURSUING** ORLICK AT THAT TIME. BY DETAINING US THERE, SUCH A COURSE MIGHT BE **FATAL** TO **PROVIS.** ON GAINING THE TOWN, I PRESENTED TRABB'S BOY WITH TWO **GUINEAS** AND TOLD HIM THAT I WAS **SORRY** EVER TO HAVE HAD AN **ILL** OPINION OF HIM.

THEY LAID IT BARE. IT WAS VIOLENTLY **SWOLLEN** AND **INFLAMED,** AND I COULD SCARCELY ENDURE TO HAVE IT **TOUCHED.**

THIS MADE NO IMPRESSION ON HIM AT **ALL.** WE WENT BACK TO LONDON THAT NIGHT, THREE IN THE POST-CHAISE.

IT WAS **DAYLIGHT** WHEN WE REACHED HOME. I WENT AT ONCE TO **BED,** AND LAY IN BED ALL DAY.

MY BURNING **ARM** THROBBED, AND MY BURNING **HEAD** THROBBED.

HERBERT AND STARTOP KEPT ME VERY **QUIET,** AND KEPT MY ARM CONSTANTLY DRESSED.

AT **LAST** I SLEPT **SOUNDLY.**

WEDNESDAY MORNING WAS DAWNING WHEN I LOOKED OUT OF THE WINDOW. I FELT **STRONG** AND **WELL**. STARTOP LAY ASLEEP ON THE SOFA. I MADE UP THE FIRE, AND GOT SOME COFFEE READY.

OF ALL MY WORLDLY **POSSESSIONS** I TOOK NO MORE THAN THE FEW **NECESSARIES** THAT FILLED A **BAG**.

IN **GOOD** TIME, HERBERT AND STARTOP **STARTED UP** STRONG AND WELL.

OUR PLAN WAS **THIS**. THE TIDE, BEGINNING TO RUN **DOWN** AT NINE, AND BEING WITH US UNTIL THREE, WE INTENDED TO **CREEP** ON AFTER IT HAD TURNED, AND ROW **AGAINST** IT UNTIL **DARK**. WE SHOULD THEN BE WELL BELOW **GRAVESEND**, WHERE THE RIVER IS **BROAD** AND **SOLITARY**.

WE SHOULD LIE BY IN A LONELY **TAVERN** FOR THE **NIGHT**, AND AWAIT THE **STEAMERS** THAT WOULD START FROM LONDON ON **THURSDAY** MORNING.

FAITHFUL **DEAR** BOY; WELL **DONE**.

THANKYE, **THANKYE!**

I LOOKED **WARILY** FOR ANY TOKEN OF OUR BEING **SUSPECTED**. I SAW **NONE**. WE WERE CERTAINLY NOT FOLLOWED BY ANY BOAT. I FELT MORTIFIED TO BE OF SO LITTLE **USE** IN THE BOAT, BUT MY FRIENDS ROWED WITH A STEADY STROKE.

NIGHT **FELL**, AND STILL WE ROWED ON FOR FOUR OR FIVE DULL **MILES**. AT LENGTH WE DESCRIED THE LIGHT OF A LONELY **PUBLIC-HOUSE**, AND RAN ALONGSIDE A LITTLE CAUSEWAY. I STEPPED **ASHORE**.

IT WAS A **DIRTY** PLACE ENOUGH, BUT THERE WAS A **FIRE** IN THE KITCHEN, EGGS AND BACON TO **EAT**, AND TWO DOUBLE-BEDDED **ROOMS**.

WE WERE UP **EARLY**, AND ROWED OUT INTO THE TRACK OF THE STEAMER. IT WAS HALF-PAST ONE BEFORE WE SAW HER **SMOKE**, AND BEHIND IT THE SMOKE OF **ANOTHER** STEAMER.

AS THEY WERE COMING ON AT FULL **SPEED**, WE GOT THE BAGS **READY**. WE HAD ALL SHAKEN HANDS CORDIALLY...

...WHEN I SAW A FOUR-OARED **GALLEY** SHOOT OUT FROM UNDER THE **BANK** A LITTLE WAY AHEAD, AND ROW OUT INTO THE **SAME** TRACK.

THE GALLEY **CROSSED** US AND FELL **ALONGSIDE**. THE HAMBURG STEAMER WAS ALMOST **UPON** US, WHEN THE GALLEY **HAILED**:

YOU HAVE A RETURNED **TRANSPORT** THERE.

THAT'S THE MAN, WRAPPED IN THE **CLOAK**. HIS NAME IS **ABEL MAGWITCH**, OTHERWISE **PROVIS**.

I **APPREHEND** THAT MAN, AND CALL UPON HIM TO **SURRENDER**, AND YOU TO **ASSIST**.

IT WAS BUT FOR AN **INSTANT** THAT I SEEMED TO **STRUGGLE** WITH A THOUSAND MILL-WEIRS AND A THOUSAND FLASHES OF LIGHT;

THAT INSTANT **PAST**, I WAS TAKEN ON BOARD THE GALLEY. **HERBERT** WAS THERE, AND **STARTOP** WAS THERE; BUT OUR BOAT WAS **GONE**, AND THE TWO **CONVICTS** WERE **GONE**.

EVERY MAN LOOKED **EAGERLY** AT THE WATER.

PRESENTLY A DARK OBJECT WAS SEEN **SWIMMING** TOWARDS US. AS IT CAME NEARER, I SAW IT TO BE **MAGWITCH**. HE WAS TAKEN ON BOARD, AND INSTANTLY **MANACLED**.

≈gasp≈

SPLAASH!

WE KEPT LOOK-OUT FOR THE **OTHER** CONVICT, BUT EVERYBODY KNEW THAT IT WAS **HOPELESS**. AT LENGTH WE GAVE IT UP.

WE PULLED UNDER THE SHORE TO THE TAVERN WE HAD LATELY **LEFT**. HERE I WAS ABLE TO GET SOME **COMFORTS** FOR **MAGWITCH** – PROVIS NO **LONGER** – WHO HAD RECEIVED SOME SEVERE **INJURY** IN THE CHEST, AND A DEEP CUT IN THE **HEAD**.

HE TOLD ME IN A **WHISPER** THAT HE AND COMPEYSON HAD GONE **OVERBOARD** TOGETHER. THERE HAD BEEN A STRUGGLE **UNDERWATER**, AND THEN HE HAD STRUCK OUT AND SWUM AWAY.

The SHIP

THE OFFICER GAVE ME **LEAVE** TO ACCOMPANY MAGWITCH TO **LONDON**. HERBERT AND STARTOP WERE TO RETURN BY **LAND**.

HIS **BREATHING** BECAME MORE DIFFICULT AND **PAINFUL**. I COULD NOT BE **SORRY** AT HEART FOR HIS BEING **BADLY HURT**, SINCE IT WAS UNQUESTIONABLY **BEST** THAT HE SHOULD **DIE**.

THAT HE WOULD BE **LENIENTLY** TREATED, I COULD NOT **HOPE**. HE WHO HAD RETURNED FROM **TRANSPORTATION** AND OCCASIONED THE **DEATH** OF THE MAN WHO WAS THE CAUSE OF HIS **ARREST**.

MY **REPUGNANCE** TO HIM HAD ALL **MELTED** AWAY. IN THE WOUNDED, SHACKLED CREATURE, I ONLY SAW A **MAN** WHO HAD MEANT TO BE MY **BENEFACTOR**, AND HAD BEHAVED WITH GREAT **CONSTANCY**.

AS WE RETURNED TOWARDS THE SETTING SUN, I TOLD HIM HOW **GRIEVED** I WAS TO THINK THAT HE HAD COME **HOME** FOR MY **SAKE**.

DEAR BOY; I'M **QUITE** CONTENT TO TAKE MY CHANCE. BUT LOOK'EE **HERE**, IT'S BEST AS A GENTLEMAN SHOULD NOT BE KNOWED TO BELONG TO **ME** NOW. ONLY COME TO SEE ME AS IF YOU COME BY **CHANCE** ALONGER WEMMICK.

I WILL NEVER **STIR** FROM YOUR **SIDE** WHEN I AM SUFFERED TO BE **NEAR** YOU.

PLEASE GOD, I WILL BE AS **TRUE** TO **YOU** AS YOU HAVE BEEN TO **ME**!

IT PUT INTO MY MIND A **THOUGHT**: THAT HE NEED NEVER KNOW HOW HIS HOPES OF **ENRICHING** ME HAD **PERISHED**.

HE WAS TAKEN TO THE POLICE COURT NEXT DAY. HE WOULD HAVE BEEN *IMMEDIATELY* COMMITTED FOR *TRIAL*, BUT THAT IT WAS NECESSARY TO SEND FOR AN OLD OFFICER OF THE PRISON-SHIP TO *IDENTIFY* HIM.

I WENT TO MR. JAGGERS TO RETAIN HIS ASSISTANCE, BUT HE TOLD ME THAT THE CASE WOULD BE *OVER* IN FIVE MINUTES WHEN THE *WITNESS* WAS THERE.

WHEN CONVICTED, MAGWITCH'S *POSSESSIONS* WOULD BE *FORFEITED* TO THE *CROWN*. BUT IN HIS IGNORANCE, POOR FELLOW, HE NEVER MISTRUSTED BUT THAT MY *INHERITANCE* WAS *SAFE*. I IMPARTED TO MR. JAGGERS MY DESIGN OF KEEPING HIM *IGNORANT* OF THE *FATE* OF HIS WEALTH.

AFTER THREE DAYS, THE WITNESS CAME, AND HE WAS COMMITTED TO TRIAL AT THE NEXT SESSIONS.

AT THIS *DARK* TIME, HERBERT RETURNED HOME ONE EVENING CAST *DOWN*.

MY DEAR HANDEL, I FEAR I SHALL SOON HAVE TO *LEAVE* YOU. WE SHALL LOSE A FINE *OPPORTUNITY* IF I PUT OFF GOING TO CAIRO, AND I AM AFRAID I *MUST* GO, WHEN YOU MOST *NEED* ME.

IN THIS BRANCH HOUSE OF OURS, HANDEL, WE MUST HAVE A – A *CLERK*. AND I HOPE IT IS NOT *UNLIKELY* THAT HE MAY EXPAND INTO A *PARTNER*. IN SHORT, MY DEAR BOY; WILL YOU *COME* TO ME?

IF YOU THOUGHT YOU COULD LEAVE THE QUESTION *OPEN* FOR A *LITTLE* WHILE...

FOR *ANY* WHILE – SIX MONTHS, A *YEAR*!

ON THE SATURDAY IN THAT SAME WEEK, I TOOK MY *LEAVE* OF HERBERT AS HE SAT ON ONE OF THE SEAPORT MAIL COACHES. I WENT TO MY *LONELY* HOME, TO ENCOUNTER *WEMMICK*. I HAD NOT SEEN HIM ALONE SINCE THE *DISASTROUS* ATTEMPTED *FLIGHT*.

IT'S A *BAD* JOB, AND I HAVEN'T BEEN SO CUT UP FOR A *LONG* TIME. WHAT I LOOK AT IS THE SACRIFICE OF SO *MUCH* PORTABLE *PROPERTY*.

I THINK OF THE POOR *OWNER* OF THE PROPERTY.

TO BE *SURE*. BUT THE LATE COMPEYSON HAVING INTELLIGENCE OF HIS *RETURN*, AND BEING SO *DETERMINED* TO BRING HIM TO *BOOK*, I DO NOT THINK HE COULD HAVE BEEN *SAVED*.

YOU DON'T BLAME *ME*, I HOPE, MR. PIP? I AM SURE I *TRIED* TO SERVE YOU, WITH *ALL* MY *HEART*.

I AM *SURE* OF THAT, AND THANK YOU MOST EARNESTLY FOR YOUR *FRIENDSHIP*.

I AM TAKING A *HOLIDAY* ON MONDAY, MR. PIP. I'M GOING TO TAKE A *WALK*, AND I'M GOING TO ASK YOU TO TAKE IT WITH ME. I KNOW YOU ARE OUT OF SORTS, BUT IF YOU COULD *OBLIGE* ME, I SHOULD TAKE IT AS A KINDNESS.

IT AIN'T A *LONG* WALK, AND IT'S AN *EARLY* ONE.

AS HE HAD DONE SO *MUCH* FOR ME, I SAID I WOULD MANAGE IT.

HE LAY IN PRISON VERY *ILL* DURING THE INTERVAL BETWEEN HIS COMMITTAL FOR TRIAL AND THE SESSIONS. HE HAD *BROKEN* TWO *RIBS*, THEY HAD WOUNDED ONE OF HIS *LUNGS*, AND HE *BREATHED* WITH GREAT *DIFFICULTY*.

BEING TOO ILL TO REMAIN IN THE COMMON *PRISON*, HE WAS REMOVED INTO THE *INFIRMARY*. THIS GAVE ME OPPORTUNITIES OF BEING WITH HIM THAT I COULD NOT *OTHERWISE* HAVE HAD.

DAY BY DAY, HE *WASTED* AND BECAME *WEAKER*, FROM THE DAY WHEN THE PRISON DOOR *CLOSED* UPON HIM.

WHEN THE SESSIONS CAME ROUND, THE *TRIAL* CAME ON AT ONCE, AND HE WAS PUT TO THE BAR, SEATED IN A CHAIR. THE TRIAL WAS *VERY SHORT*.

SUCH THINGS AS COULD BE SAID FOR HIM WERE SAID, BUT NOTHING COULD UNSAY THE FACT THAT HE HAD *RETURNED*. IT WAS *IMPOSSIBLE* TO DO *OTHERWISE* THAN FIND HIM *GUILTY*.

AT THAT TIME, IT WAS THE *CUSTOM* TO DEVOTE A CONCLUDING DAY TO THE PASSING OF *SENTENCES* AND THE *SENTENCE OF DEATH*.

TWO-AND-THIRTY MEN AND WOMEN CAME BEFORE THE JUDGE TO RECEIVE *THAT* SENTENCE *TOGETHER*.

FOREMOST AMONG THE TWO-AND-THIRTY WAS *HE*.

THE JUDGE ADDRESSED THEM. AMONG THE WRETCHED CREATURES BEFORE HIM, HE SINGLED OUT FOR **SPECIAL** ADDRESS, ONE WHO ALMOST FROM HIS INFANCY HAD BEEN AN **OFFENDER**; WHO HAD BEEN AT LENGTH SENTENCED TO **EXILE**, BUT WHO HAD COME **BACK**.

...THE APPOINTED **PUNISHMENT** BEING **DEATH**, YOU MUST PREPARE YOURSELF TO **DIE**.

MY LORD, I HAVE RECEIVED MY SENTENCE OF **DEATH** FROM THE **ALMIGHTY**; BUT I BOW TO **YOURS**.

FOR SEVERAL NIGHTS AFTER HE WAS SENTENCED I TOOK **NO** REST EXCEPT WHEN I FELL ASLEEP IN MY CHAIR. MY DAILY VISITS WERE **SHORTENED** NOW, AND HE WAS MORE STRICTLY KEPT; BUT NOBODY WAS HARD WITH HIM OR ME.

THE OFFICER ALWAYS GAVE ME THE ASSURANCE THAT HE WAS **WORSE**.

AS THE DAYS WENT ON, I NOTICED THAT HE WOULD LIE **PLACIDLY** LOOKING AT THE CEILING. TEN DAYS AFTER THE SENTENCE, I SAW A **GREATER** CHANGE IN HIM THAN I HAD SEEN YET.

Dear boy, I thought you was **late**. But I knowed you **couldn't** be that.

IT IS JUST THE **TIME**. I WAITED FOR IT AT THE GATE.

You always **waits** at the gate; don't you, dear boy?

God **bless** you! You've never **deserted** me, dear boy.

ARE YOU IN **MUCH** PAIN TODAY?

I don't **complain** of none, dear boy.

YOU NEVER **DO** COMPLAIN.

HE HAD SPOKEN HIS **LAST WORDS**. HE **SMILED**, AND I UNDERSTOOD THAT HE WISHED TO LIFT MY HAND, AND LAY IT ON HIS BREAST.

THE ALLOTTED **TIME** RAN OUT, BUT THE OFFICER LET ME **STAY**.

NOW THAT I WAS LEFT WHOLLY TO **MYSELF**, I GAVE NOTICE OF MY INTENTION TO **QUIT** THE CHAMBERS IN THE TEMPLE. I WAS IN **DEBT**, AND HAD SCARCELY ANY **MONEY**.

I SHOULD HAVE BEEN SERIOUSLY **ALARMED** BY THIS STATE OF AFFAIRS, BUT FOR THE FACT THAT I PERCEIVED THAT I WAS FALLING **VERY ILL**.

FOR A DAY OR TWO, I LAY ON THE **SOFA**, OR ON THE **FLOOR**, ACCORDING AS I HAPPENED TO SINK DOWN, WITH A HEAVY HEAD, ACHING LIMBS, AND NO **PURPOSE** OR **POWER**.

THEN THERE CAME ONE NIGHT OF GREAT **DURATION**, WHICH TEEMED WITH ANXIETY AND **HORROR**. IN THE MORNING WHEN I TRIED TO **SIT UP**, I FOUND I COULD **NOT** DO SO.

AT LAST, THROUGH A **VAPOUR**, I SAW **TWO MEN** LOOKING AT ME.

WHAT DO YOU **WANT?** I DON'T **KNOW** YOU.

WELL, SIR, I DARE SAY THIS IS A MATTER THAT YOU'LL SOON **ARRANGE**, BUT YOU'RE **ARRESTED**.

THE **DEBT** IS ONE HUNDRED AND TWENTY-THREE POUND, FIFTEEN AND SIX. **JEWELLER'S** ACCOUNT.

YOU HAD BETTER COME TO MY **HOUSE** – I KEEP A **NICE** HOUSE.

THEY **FORBORE** TO REMOVE ME. THEN I HAD A FEVER AND OFTEN **LOST MY REASON**.

I WAS BESET BY FEVERED VISIONS. THE TIME SEEMED **INTERMINABLE**, BUT EVENTUALLY I **TURNED** THE WORST POINT OF MY ILLNESS.

ONE DAY I **OPENED** MY EYES AND **SAW**, IN THE CHAIR AT THE BEDSIDE...

IS IT **JOE?**

WHICH IT **AIR**, OLD CHAP.

HOW **LONG**, DEAR JOE?

WHICH YOU MEANTERSAY, PIP, HOW LONG HAVE YOUR **ILLNESS** LASTED?

IT'S THE END OF **MAY**, OLD CHAP.

FOR, AS I SAYS TO BIDDY WHEN THE **NEWS** OF YOUR BEING ILL WERE BROUGHT BY **LETTER**, THAT HOW YOU MIGHT BE AMONGST **STRANGERS**, AND THAT A WIS/T AT SUCH A MOMENT MIGHT NOT PROVE **UNACCEPTABOBBLE**. AND BIDDY, HER WORD WERE, *"GO TO HIM, WITHOUT LOSS OF TIME."*

THE TIDINGS OF MY **FORTUNES** HAVING HAD A HEAVY **FALL** HAD GOT DOWN TO MY NATIVE PLACE **BEFORE** I GOT THERE.

WHEN I ARRIVED, MUCH **FATIGUED** BY THE JOURNEY, THE BOAR COULD ONLY ASSIGN ME AN **INDIFFERENT** CHAMBER UP THE YARD. BUT I HAD AS SOUND A SLEEP THERE AS IN THE **BEST** BEDROOM.

EARLY IN THE MORNING, BEFORE BREAKFAST, I STROLLED ROUND BY SATIS HOUSE. THERE WERE PRINTED **BILLS** ON THE GATE, ANNOUNCING A **SALE** BY AUCTION OF THE HOUSEHOLD FURNITURE AND EFFECTS NEXT WEEK.

THE HOUSE **ITSELF** WAS TO BE **SOLD** AND **PULLED DOWN.**

WHEN I GOT **BACK** TO MY BREAKFAST, I FOUND **MR. PUMBLECHOOK** CONVERSING WITH THE LANDLORD.

YOUNG MAN, I AM **SORRY** TO SEE YOU BROUGHT LOW. BUT WHAT **ELSE** COULD BE EXPECTED! AND HAS IT COME TO **THIS!**

AND AIR YOU A GOING TO **JOSEPH?**

IN HEAVEN'S NAME, WHAT DOES IT **MATTER** TO **YOU** WHERE I AM **GOING?**

FOR ONCE YOU ARE **RIGHT.** I **FORGIT** MYSELF WHEN I TAKE SUCH AN **INTEREST.** AND YET, THIS IS **HIM** AS I EVER SPORTED WITH IN HIS DAYS OF HAPPY **INFANCY!**

THIS IS **HIM** AS I HAVE SEEN BROUGHT UP BY **HAND.** LET HIM **DENY** IT IF HE CAN!

WITH THOSE WORDS THE **IMPOSTOR** LEFT, SHAKING HIS HEAD IN **DISAPPROVAL.**

I WENT **SOFTLY** TOWARDS THE FORGE, MEANING TO PEEP OVER THE FLOWERS, WHEN JOE AND BIDDY STOOD BEFORE ME, **ARM IN ARM.**
BIDDY GAVE A **CRY**, AND IN ANOTHER **MOMENT** SHE WAS IN MY **EMBRACE.**

BUT DEAR **BIDDY**, HOW **SMART** YOU ARE! AND JOE, HOW SMART **YOU** ARE!

YES, DEAR PIP.

IT'S MY **WEDDING DAY**, AND I AM **MARRIED** TO **JOE!**

WHICH HE WARN'T **STRONG** ENOUGH, MY DEAR, FUR TO BE **SURPRISED**.

I OUGHT TO HAVE **THOUGHT** OF IT, DEAR JOE, BUT I WAS TOO **HAPPY**.

DEAR BIDDY, YOU HAVE THE BEST **HUSBAND** IN THE WHOLE WORLD! AND, DEAR JOE, YOU HAVE THE BEST **WIFE** IN THE WHOLE WORLD!

AND JOE AND BIDDY **BOTH**, RECEIVE MY HUMBLE **THANKS** FOR ALL YOU HAVE **DONE** FOR ME, AND ALL I HAVE SO **ILL** REPAID!

I AM SOON GOING **ABROAD**, AND SHALL NEVER **REST** UNTIL I HAVE WORKED FOR THE **MONEY** WITH WHICH YOU HAVE KEPT ME OUT OF **PRISON**.

BUT I MUST SAY **MORE**. DEAR JOE, I HOPE YOU WILL HAVE **CHILDREN** TO LOVE, AND THAT SOME LITTLE FELLOW WILL SIT IN THIS CHIMNEY-CORNER OF A WINTER NIGHT, WHO MAY **REMIND** YOU OF ANOTHER LITTLE FELLOW GONE **FOR EVER**.

DON'T **TELL** HIM, JOE, THAT I WAS **THANKLESS**. DON'T TELL HIM, BIDDY, THAT I WAS **UNGENEROUS** AND **UNJUST**.

ONLY TELL HIM THAT I **HONOURED** YOU **BOTH** BECAUSE YOU WERE SO GOOD AND **TRUE**.

AND NOW, PRAY TELL ME, **BOTH**, THAT YOU **FORGIVE** ME, THAT I MAY CARRY THE SOUND **AWAY** WITH ME!

O DEAR OLD **PIP**, GOD **KNOWS** AS I **FORGIVE** YOU, IF I HAVE **ANYTHINK** TO FORGIVE!

AMEN! GOD KNOWS **I DO**!

I SOLD **ALL** I HAD FOR A **COMPOSITION** WITH MY CREDITORS. WITHIN A MONTH, I HAD **QUITTED** ENGLAND, AND WITHIN TWO MONTHS I WAS CLERK TO CLARRIKER AND Cº.

SOON I ASSUMED MY FIRST **RESPONSIBILITY**, FOR THE PARLOUR CEILING AT MILL POND BANK HAD CEASED TO **TREMBLE** UNDER BILL BARLEY'S GROWLS, AND FOR HERBERT WENT AWAY TO **MARRY** CLARA. I WAS LEFT IN **CHARGE** OF THE EASTERN BRANCH UNTIL HE CAME BACK.

MANY A **YEAR** WENT ROUND BEFORE I WAS A PARTNER IN THE HOUSE; BUT I LIVED **HAPPILY** WITH HERBERT AND HIS WIFE. I LIVED **FRUGALLY**, AND MAINTAINED A CORRESPONDENCE WITH BIDDY AND JOE.

WHEN I BECAME **THIRD** IN THE FIRM, CLARRIKER BETRAYED MY **SECRET** TO HERBERT, AND HERBERT WAS AS MUCH **MOVED** AS **AMAZED**.

WE WERE NEVER A **GREAT** HOUSE, BUT WE WORKED FOR OUR PROFITS, AND DID VERY **WELL**.

FOR **ELEVEN** YEARS, I HAD NOT SEEN JOE NOR BIDDY; WHEN, ONE EVENING IN DECEMBER, I RAISED THE **LATCH** OF THE KITCHEN DOOR, AND LOOKED IN **UNSEEN.**

THERE, IN THE OLD PLACE BY THE FIRE SAT JOE; AND THERE, SITTING ON MY **OWN** LITTLE STOOL WAS – I AGAIN!

WE GIV' HIM THE NAME OF **PIP** FOR **YOUR** SAKE, DEAR OLD CHAP, AND WE THINK HE GROW A LITTLE BIT **LIKE** YOU.

BIDDY, YOU MUST GIVE PIP TO **ME** ONE OF THESE DAYS; OR **LEND** HIM, AT ALL EVENTS.

NO, NO, YOU MUST **MARRY.**

SO HERBERT AND CLARA SAY, BUT I DON'T THINK I **SHALL**, BIDDY. I HAVE SO **SETTLED DOWN** IN THEIR HOME, AND AM **ALREADY** QUITE AN OLD **BACHELOR.**

DEAR PIP. YOU ARE **SURE** YOU DON'T **FRET** FOR HER?

O NO – I THINK **NOT**, BIDDY.

TELL ME AS AN OLD **FRIEND**. HAVE YOU QUITE **FORGOTTEN** HER?

DEAR BIDDY, I HAVE FORGOTTEN **NOTHING** IN MY LIFE THAT EVER HAD A **FOREMOST** PLACE THERE. BUT THAT **POOR DREAM**, AS I ONCE USED TO CALL IT, HAS **ALL** GONE BY.

NEVERTHELESS, I KNEW, WHILE I **SAID** THOSE WORDS, THAT I INTENDED TO **REVISIT** THE SITE OF THE OLD HOUSE THAT EVENING FOR **HER** SAKE. **YES**, FOR ESTELLA'S SAKE.

I HAD HEARD OF ESTELLA AS LEADING A MOST **UNHAPPY** LIFE, AND AS BEING **SEPARATED** FROM HER HUSBAND, WHO HAD USED HER WITH GREAT **CRUELTY.** HE WAS QUITE **RENOWNED** AS A COMPOUND OF PRIDE, AVARICE, BRUTALITY, AND MEANNESS.

AND I HAD HEARD OF HIS **DEATH**, FROM AN ACCIDENT CONSEQUENT ON HIS **ILL-TREATMENT** OF A HORSE.

THIS RELEASE HAD **BEFALLEN** SOME TWO YEARS BEFORE; FOR ANYTHING I KNEW, SHE WAS **MARRIED** AGAIN.

GREAT EXPECTATIONS

The End

Editor's Note:

The last phrase is taken from the revised ending that Dickens wrote for the first single-volume edition of 1862. It is intentionally ambiguous — probably more so than the previously published version of the phrase, which was, "I saw the shadow of no parting from her." However, because Dickens himself obviously felt that the 1862 ending was an improvement, we felt justified to use that phrase for this adaptation.

Charles Dickens

(1812 - 1870)

Charles Dickens was born was born in Landport, Portsmouth (on the south cost of England) on February 7, 1812. He was the second of eight children born to John and Elizabeth Dickens. Financially, the Dickens family were comfortable, and when they moved to Chatham, Kent in 1817 they sent Charles to a nearby private school.

By the time he was ten, the family had moved again, this time to London, following the career of his father, John, who was a clerk in the Naval Pay Office. John got into debt and was eventually sent to Marshalsea Prison in 1824. His wife and most of the children joined him there (a common occurrence in those days); Charles, however, was put to work at Warren's Blacking Factory, where he labeled jars of boot polish.

When John's mother died soon after, she left enough money to pay off the debts and reunite the family. Although brief, Charles's time at the factory haunted him for the rest of his life:

"For many years, when I came near to Robert Warren's, in the Strand, I crossed over to the opposite side of the way, to avoid a certain smell of the cement they put upon the blacking corks, which reminded me of what I once was. My old way home by the borough made me cry, after my oldest child could speak."

© V&A Images, Victoria and Albert Museum

Charles Dickens

Charles left school at fifteen and worked as an office boy with a Mr. Molloy of Lincoln's Inn. It was here that Charles made the decision to become a journalist. He studied shorthand at night and went on to spend two years as a shorthand reporter at the Doctors' Commons Courts.

From 1830 to 1836 he wrote for a number of newspapers; he also started to achieve recognition for his own written work. In December 1833 his first published (but unpaid for) story, "A Dinner at Poplar Walk", appeared in *The Old Monthly* magazine. About seeing his first work in print, Dickens wrote:

"On which occasion I walked down to Westminster-hall, and turned into it for half an hour, because my eyes were so dimmed with joy and pride, that they could not bear the street, and were not fit to be seen there".

He wrote further stories for *The Old Monthly*; but when the magazine could not pay for them, Dickens began to write his "series" for *The Chronicle* at the request of the editor, George Hogarth.

In 1835, Charles got engaged to George Hogarth's eldest daughter, Catherine. They married on April 2, 1836 and went on to have ten children (seven boys and three girls). Biographers have long suspected that Charles preferred Catherine's sister, Mary, who lived with the Dickens family and died in his arms in 1837 at the age of seventeen. Dickens had asked to be buried next to her; but when her brother died in 1841, Dickens's "place" was taken. He wrote to his great friend and biographer, John Forster:

> "It is a great trial for me to give up Mary's grave… the desire to be buried next to her is as strong upon me now, as it was five years ago… And I know…that it will never diminish…I cannot bear the thought of being excluded from her dust".

The first series of *Sketches by Boz* was published in 1836 ("Boz" was an early pen name used by Dickens). Shortly afterwards, with the success of *Pickwick Papers* in 1837, Dickens was at last a full-time novelist. He produced works at an incredible rate; and at the start of his writing career he also managed to continue his work as a journalist and editor. He began his next book, *Oliver Twist*, in 1837 and continued it in monthly parts until April 1839.

Dickens visited Canada and the United States in 1842. During that visit he spoke on the need for international copyright, because some American publishers were printing his books without his permission and without making any payment; he also talked about the need to end slavery. His visit and his opinions were recorded and published as *American Notes* in October of that year, causing quite a stir.

On December 17, 1843 his much-loved Christmas tale, *A Christmas Carol* (also available as a Classical Comics graphic novel) was published. It was so popular that it sold five-thousand copies by Christmas Eve – and has never been out of print since.

From childhood, Dickens had loved the stage and enjoyed the attention and applause he received. He performed in amateur theater throughout the 1840s and 50s, and he formed his own amateur theatrical company in 1845, which occupied much of his time.

Dickens became something of an international celebrity. In 1853 he toured Italy, and on his return to England, he gave the first of many public readings from his own works. At first he did these for charity, but before long he demanded payment.

By 1856, Dickens had made enough money to purchase a fine country house: Gads Hill in Kent. Although he had admired this place ever since his arrival in the area as a child, it was not to be a happy family home. A year later, Charles met a young actress called Ellen Lawless Ternan who went on to join his theater company; and they began a relationship that was to last until his death.

Charles separated from his wife Catherine in 1858. The event was talked about in the newspapers, and Dickens publicly denied rumors of an affair. He was morally trapped — he was deeply in love with Ellen, but his writing career was based on promoting family values and being a good person; he felt that if he admitted his relationship with Ellen, it would put an end to his career.

Catherine moved to a house in London with their eldest son Charles, and Dickens remained at Gads Hill with the rest of the children and Catherine's sister, Georgina (there were rumours of Charles and Georgina having a relationship, too).

The more he tried to hide his personal life, the more it came out in his writing. *Great Expectations* was written around this time (1860) and includes elements of all the emotions he was experiencing: imprisonment, love that can never be, people living in isolation, and the compulsion to better oneself. He continued to look after Ellen

and made regular secret journeys to see her — not easy for the local celebrity that Dickens had become. He went to incredible lengths to keep his secret safe, including renting houses under different names and setting up offices for his business in places that made it easy for him to visit her.

In 1865, Dickens was involved in the Staplehurst Rail Crash, an incident which disturbed him greatly. He was travelling with Ellen and her mother, most likely returning from a secret holiday in France. The train left the track, resulting in the deaths of ten people and injuries to forty more. It is reported that Dickens tended to some of the wounded.

By 1867 Dickens's health was getting worse. His doctor advised him to rest, but he carried on with his busy schedule, which included a second tour of America.

He returned to England and, despite his bad health, continued his work and his public reading appearances. In April 1869, he collapsed during a reading at

Preston, and he was again advised to rest. Dickens didn't listen. He continued to give performances in London, and he even started work on a new novel, *The Mystery of Edwin Drood*. This novel was never finished: he suffered a stroke and died suddenly at Gads Hill on June 9, 1870. He had asked to be buried "in an inexpensive, unostentatious, and strictly private manner" but public opinion, led by *The Times* newspaper, insisted that he should be buried in keeping with his status as a great writer. He was buried at Westminster Abbey on June 14, 1870.

His funeral was a private affair, attended by just twelve mourners. After the service, his grave was left open and thousands of people from all walks of life came to pay their respects and throw flowers onto the coffin. Today, a small stone with a simple inscription marks his grave:

"CHARLES DICKENS
BORN 7th FEBRUARY 1812
DIED 9th JUNE 1870"

The Dickens Family Tree

Key:
Parent of ———
Married ═══

| William Dickens d. 1785 | Elizabeth Ball d. 1824 | Charles Barrow *m. 1788* 1759–1826 | Mary Culliford 1771–1851 |

Mary Barrow ?

Thomas Culliford Barrow 1793–1857

Other children

| William Dickens 1783–1826 | John Dickens *m. 1809* 1785–1851 | Elizabeth Barrow 1789–1863 |

Frances Elizabeth Dickens 1810–1848

Alfred Dickens b. & d. 1814

Letitia Mary Dickens 1816–1874

Harriet Ellen Dickens b. & d. 1819

Frederick William Dickens 1820–1868

Alfred Lamerte Dickens 1822–1860

Augustus Dickens 1827–1868

George Hogarth *m. 1814* 1783–1870

Georgina Thomson 1793–1863

Charles John Huffam Dickens *m. 1836* 1812–1870

Catherine Thomson Hogarth 1815–1879

Mary Hogarth 1819–1837

Georgina Hogarth 1827–1917

Other children

Charles Culliford Boz Dickens 1837–1896

Kate Macready Dickens 1839–1929

Francis Jeffrey Dickens 1844–1886

Sydney Smith Haldimand Dickens 1847–1872

Dora Annie Dickens 1850–1851

Mary Dickens 1838–1896

Walter Landor Dickens 1841–1863

Alfred Tennyson Dickens 1845–1912

Henry Fielding Dickens 1849–1933

Edward Bulwer Lytton Dickens 1852–1902

Due to the lack of official records of births, deaths and marriages within this period, the above information is derived from extensive research and is as accurate as possible from the limited sources available.

Crime and Punishment

A strong thread of criminality runs throughout *Great Expectations*, much as it did in everyday Victorian London. Dickens himself was of course no stranger to the "wrong side of the law". As a young man, his father served time as an insolvent debtor in Marshalsea Prison, and for a while Charles worked as a court reporter. He also lived in a time of great social change, brought about by the increase in population, the impact of technological advances, the rise of industry, and the development of travel and transportation; but it was also a time of increasing crime.

Elizabeth Fry

The most notable prison reformer of the nineteenth century was Elizabeth Fry. Born in Norwich in 1780, she decided while still a teenager to devote her life to helping people in need. At first, she did this by giving clothes to the poor, visiting the sick, and running a Sunday School in her house where she taught children to read. Then she received her life's calling when she heard reports from a friend about the conditions in Newgate Prison (see opposite). Visiting the prison for herself in 1813, she found around three hundred women and their children huddled together in two wards and two cells. They were forced to sleep on the floor without any nightclothes or bedding, and some of them were still awaiting their trial (and therefore may well have been innocent).

She visited Newgate on a regular basis, supplying clothing and establishing a school and a chapel there. She also made sure that the women were kept occupied with sewing duties and Bible reading to help in their reformation.

In 1818, she was invited to speak to a House of Commons Committee on London Prisons. She told them how women slept thirty to a room in Newgate, where there were:

> "old and young, hardened offenders with those who had committed only a minor offence or their first crime; the lowest of women with respectable married women and maid-servants".

The committee was impressed with her work, but they disapproved of her views on capital punishment, which she said was "evil and produced evil results". Consequently, little was done.

However, in 1823 the new Home Secretary Sir Robert Peel (most famous for the introduction of the Metropolitan Police Force, also called "Peelers", and later "Bobbies") introduced *The Gaols Act*, which put some of Fry's recommendations into effect; but her work didn't stop there. The Act did not apply to local town gaols (jails) or debtors' prisons (like the one Dickens's father was sent to), and in 1820, Fry published a book which detailed the ongoing problems.

Although she was mostly concerned with prison reform, she also campaigned to help the homeless, to improve the conditions in hospitals and mental asylums, and called for reforms to the workhouses. Elizabeth Fry's training school for nurses was a big influence on Florence Nightingale's work, and she even met with Queen Victoria on several occasions. Elizabeth Fry died in 1845.

Newgate Prison

Newgate Prison features heavily in *Great Expectations*; not only because it was the principle prison in London but also because it was regarded as the symbol of crime itself.

The term "Newgate" stems from the days when London was a Roman walled city with eight entrance gates, which also included Ludgate, Bishopsgate and Aldgate — names which have survived in street names to the present day. There had been a prison on the site since the twelfth century. The Great Fire of 1667 destroyed the prison building there at the time, and a new one "of great magnificence" was built in its place. This itself was destroyed by the anti-Catholic "Gordon Rioters" in 1780, when they attacked buildings that represented law and order, and in the process freed around four hundred prisoners. The prison was rebuilt right away using a new design that incorporated three areas, one for each group of prisoners: debtors, male felons and female felons. Debtors were effectively the only long-term inmates at the prison; the male and female felons were only held there while awaiting trial, execution or transportation to the colonies. As detailed overleaf, prisoners awaiting transportation were mostly held in Prison Hulks that were moored on the River Thames until they received a place on a ship bound for Australia.

The population was increasing, especially in the cities, and this led to extreme poverty, forcing many into a life of crime. In an effort to control the rising crime figures, the government decided to strengthen the law, making many crimes punishable by death (see next page).

As a further deterrent and as a reminder of the law to others, condemned prisoners were hanged in public. Hangings took place at Tyburn, which is near where Marble Arch stands today. "Hanging Days", or "Tyburn Fairs" as they became known, were a renowned, gruesome spectacle. There were eight of them each year, and they were treated as public holidays. Crowds would gather outside Newgate Prison while a bell rang out. Carts would then take the condemned to Saint Sepulchre's Church so that they could be given their "last rites", and from there they would be taken to Tyburn to be hanged from the gallows. The public would follow them and become more rowdy and riotous as the journey progressed, rising to a fever pitch when they finally reached the scaffold.

These "Hanging Day" processions themselves posed a threat to law and order, so in 1783 when Newgate Prison was rebuilt it was decided that public hangings would take place in the street outside the prison to avoid having to move the prisoners and incite the public (the Newgate Prison gallows are mentioned in Volume II, Chapter XIII of *Great Expectations*, and appear on page 79 of this book).

Hangings remained public events until 1868, when protests by many, including Dickens, put a halt to these terrible spectacles. Newgate Prison remained in operation until the turn of the century. In 1902, along with the nearby court rooms, it was finally demolished to make way for the Old Bailey. In all, 1120 men and 49 women were hanged there, mostly for burglary, forgery or murder.

The Death Penalty

With the rising crime figures that were a consequence of the abject poverty, the government decided to increase the severity of the law — and particularly the punishment for petty crimes such as theft.

Theft of property under the value of forty shillings (two pre-decimal pounds) carried a seven-year prison sentence; theft over that amount was punishable by hanging.

However, not everyone who received the death penalty was executed. Hangings took place in public and were attended by hundreds of people; but before long, the public started to view the condemned as heroic martyrs instead of criminals.

Consequently, the number of hangings had to be reduced.

After receiving the death sentence in the courts, the Court Recorder would prepare his report to the King and Privy Council. In that report, he would indicate which prisoners should hang and which should be granted reprieve. Murderers were hanged within two days of sentencing, but other

criminals had to wait in prison for up to four months to hear their fate. It was quite common for female prisoners to claim that they were pregnant (which they often were!) and force a reprieve that way. Instead of being hanged, prisoners who were granted reprieve were selected for transportation (see below).

Transportation

The idea to ship criminals out of Britain started life nearly two hundred years before Dickens was born (and while Shakespeare was still alive). In 1597, an act was

passed to "banish dangerous criminals from the Kingdom"; but it took until 1615 for the first convict ships to leave England. Back then, they were sent to America. This continued for over a hundred and fifty years; but with the War of Independence in 1775, the American colonies closed their ports to British prison ships, and a new destination had to be found. The government decided upon New South Wales (Australia), and the first 778 convicts (586 male, 192 female) left Britain in 1787.

The area formally became a British Colony in 1788, and from then until 1868 when transportation ended, 165,000 convicts were sent there, with only one-in-eight of these being female.

Surprisingly, despite the incredibly long journey of six to twelve months on crowded ships, few prisoners (fewer than one-in-twenty) died during the voyage. In fact, like Abel Magwitch in this book, many prisoners endured only a short period of confinement or labour, after which they were released "on licence". Although they could not return to Britain, many went on to prosper in their new home.

Prison Hulks

When transportation to America came to an abrupt halt in 1775, and before New South Wales became the replacement destination, a solution had to be found to house the growing number of convicts awaiting deportation. As a temporary solution, these convicts were warehoused in old warships moored in the River Thames. Bought by the prison authorities after the Royal Navy had taken them out of service, these Prison Hulks went on to become long-term fixtures where convicts were held as they waited for the next voyage that would take them away.

Hulks were soon treated as the answer to the generally overcrowded prisons, and were used to detain many prisoners who were not even due to be transported abroad; at one point, over two-thirds of all prisoners were held on hulks. Conditions on these floating prisons were even worse than those on land. One famous hulk, *The Warrior*, comprised three decks, each holding 150 to 200 convicts. The decks were divided into caged cells on both sides of the hull, with a walkway down the middle. Each cell housed eight to ten men, with only the old gun ports in the sides of the hull for ventilation.

Prisoners were forced to sleep with chains around their waists and ankles to prevent them from escaping at night. Any that were found to have made an attempt to file away or otherwise remove them were either flogged, secured with extra irons, or put in solitary confinement.

The hulks were terribly unsanitary. Not only were there problems caused by the overcrowded living conditions, but all water was taken from the polluted Thames, and this gave rise to outbreaks of many diseases, such as cholera, "Gaol Fever" (a form of typhus spread by vermin) and dysentery. Large numbers of prisoners died from these diseases.

By 1850, the use of hulks was in decline; and in 1857, the last hulk was destroyed. Although hulks were no longer in use when Dickens started to write *Great Expectations* (1860), their presence in the book is not an error. The hulks appear at the start of the book, which is set in 1812 — a time when the use of hulks was probably at their peak.

Page Creation

1. Script

The first stage is to adapt the entire story into comic book panels, describing the images to be drawn as well as the dialogue and captions. The challenge that Jen Green faced with *Great Expectations* was how to condense a 400+ page Dickens novel into 140 pages of graphic novel and still retain all the events, details, plot twists and connections. There are two versions of the dialogue and captions: Original Text and Quick Text. Both versions use the same artwork.

Page 19 from the script of *Great Expectations* showing 2 text versions.

2. Character Sheets

Before the script was completed, John Stokes began work on visualizing the characters and important scenes. Here you see his sketches of Pip and Miss Havisham. This pre-production is an important stage because it sets the tone for the whole book and enables the artist to develop the final look of the artwork.

3. Rough Sketch

Once the artist receives the script, he takes his character designs and creates rough layouts. John's "roughs" are very detailed. He is considering many things at this stage, including pacing of the action, emphasis of certain elements to tell the story in the best way, lettering space and even lighting of the scene. If any changes need to be made, then it is far easier to make them at this stage, before the page is drawn.

The rough sketch created from the script.

4. Pencils

The process to create the finished artwork begins as soon as the editor approves the rough sketch. The artwork is drawn on A3 art board at approximately 150% of the finished printed size. Because John's roughs are so detailed, very few changes are made when the page is penciled.

You can see that the tablet has been added in the first panel as a continuity from the previous page, and more lettering space was allowed for in panel 6.

Interestingly, the rough sketch details some artistic elements that won't be tackled until the coloring stage. For example, the last panel shows some night clouds in the rough, but a clear sky in the penciled page.

The pencil drawing of page 19.

5. Inks

The inking stage is important because it clarifies the pencil lines and finalizes the linework. However, inking is not simply tracing over the pencil sketch! It is more like a pre-coloring stage, in which black ink is used to fill in shaded areas and provide texture. A great example of this is in the ironwork on the water pump in panel 5.

The inked image, ready to be colored.

6. Coloring

Adding color really brings the page and its characters to life. There is far more to the coloring stage than simply replacing the white areas with flat color. Some of the linework itself is shaded, while great emphasis is placed upon texture and light sources to get realistic shadows and highlights. Effects are also considered, such as the window glass in panel 1 and the splashing water in panel 5. Finally, the whole page is color-balanced to the other pages of that scene, and to the overall book.

The final colored artwork.

7. Lettering

The final stage is to add the captions, sound effects, and speech bubbles from the script. These are laid on top of the finished colored pages. Two versions of each page are lettered, one for each of the two versions of the book (Original Text and Quick Text).

The finished page 19 with Original Text lettering.

These lettered images are then saved as final artwork pages and compiled into the finished book.

Below is a comparison showing panel 4 of page 19 in both Original Text and Quick Text versions.

Other Classics in the Series

Jane Eyre: The Graphic Novel

• 144 Pages • $16.95
• Script Adaptation: Amy Corzine • Artwork: John M. Burns • Letters: Terry Wiley

This Charlotte Brontë classic is brought to vibrant life by artist John M. Burns. His sympathetic treatment of Jane Eyre's life during the 19th century will delight any reader with its strong emotions and wonderfully rich atmosphere. Travel back to a time of grand mansions contrasted with the severest poverty and immerse yourself in this fabulous love story.

978-1-906332-47-1   978-1-906332-48-8

Frankenstein: The Graphic Novel

• 144 Pages • $16.95
• Script Adaptation: Jason Cobley • Linework: Declan Shalvey
• Colors: Jason Cardy & Kat Nicholson • Art Direction: Jon Haward • Letters: Terry Wiley

True to the original novel (rather than the square-headed Boris Karloff image from the films!) Declan's naturally gothic artistic style is a perfect match for this epic tale. Frankenstein is such a well known title, yet the films strayed so far beyond the original novel that many people today don't realize how this classic horror tale deals with such timeless subjects as alienation, empathy and understanding beyond appearance.

978-1-906332-49-5   978-1-906332-50-1

A Christmas Carol: The Graphic Novel

• 160 Pages • $16.95
• Script Adaptation: Sean Michael Wilson • Pencils: Mike Collins
• Inks: David Roach • Colors: James Offredi • Letters: Terry Wiley

A full-color graphic novel adaptation of the much-loved Christmas story from the great Charles Dickens. Set in Victorian England and highlighting the social injustice of the time, we see Ebenezer Scrooge go from oppressor to benefactor when he gets a rude awakening to how his life is, and how it should be. With sumptuous artwork and wonderful characters, this magical tale is a must-have — not only for the festive season, but all year long!

978-1-906332-51-8   978-1-906332-52-5